THE GRAYWOLF ANNUAL SIX

Stories from the Rest of the World

1 9 8 9

THE GRAYWOLF SHORT FICTION SERIES

THE GRAYWOLF
ANNUAL SIX

Stories from the
Rest of the World

EDITED BY SCOTT WALKER

GRAYWOLF PRESS · SAINT PAUL

I S B N 1-55597-122-9
I S S N 0743-7471

9 8 7 6 5 4 3 2
First Printing, 1989

Publication of this volume is made possible in part by grants from the Northwest Area Foundation, the National Endowment for the Arts and the Minnesota State Arts Board. Graywolf Press is the recipient of a McKnight Foundation Award administered by the Minnesota State Arts Board and receives generous contributions from corporations, foundations and individuals. Graywolf Press is a member agency of United Arts, Saint Paul.

Published by G R AY W O L F   P R E S S
Post Office Box 75006
Saint Paul, Minnesota 55175

TABLE OF CONTENTS

Introduction

"I have given up reading books. I find it takes my mind off myself."

—OSCAR LEVANT

I

WE, the citizens of the United States, are among the most poorly read people in the world. Our literacy rate ranks among the lowest for industrialized nations. We are not only poorly educated and relatively uninformed about United States history and culture, but our students perform miserably in tests for knowledge about world geography and history. At a time when communication between continents and cultures has become swift and amazingly easy, when business and trade are increasingly internationalized, when the need for knowledge of languages and cultures is greater than ever before in world history and in fact necessary for economic and cultural survival, the people of the United States seem peculiarly and stubbornly uninterested in anything beyond our own borders.

It is perplexing to consider the reasons why Americans remain uninterested in the world around them. Is it arrogance? Fear?

Provincialism? Racism? A sign of a culture so vital that its citizens hardly have time for themselves? Self-absorption? The effects of the myth of American world leadership, making the rest of the world seem to us irrelevant or mired in the early stages of becoming just like us? The result of lingering historical European and colonial bias?

One need go no farther than one's local bookstore for evidence of our habitual lack of interest in things outside of ourselves. We are, in the first place, not a culture that loves literature (literature being one of the best ways to engage personally in something outside of ourselves). We don't even support our own writers: American poets remind us often and wistfully that books of poetry in the Soviet Union sell as many as 200,000 copies while it is uncommon here for a book of poetry to sell more than 2,000 copies. A good book of short stories or a literary novel commonly sells fewer than 5,000 copies.

With a few exceptions – Umberto Eco's *The Name of the Rose*, Milan Kundera's *The Unbearable Lightness of Being* after the movie came out, Gabriel García Márquez, and a couple of dozen other authors translated from European languages or from Latin American editions – Americans are even less interested in fine literature in translation. Writers from principal European languages have been fairly well translated and represented in the United States, though only after they are well established abroad. Several remarkable writers from Latin America are popular here, but many of Latin America's more intellectual or difficult authors have yet to be published in the United States. Writers from "The Rest of the World" – from Africa, Asia, the Orient, Canada, non-mainstream European countries like Estonia – are almost completely unknown here.

This disinterest is unique to Americans. Most other literate cultures and countries are not only well-read in their own literature but knowledgeable about contemporary world literature. Books by some American literary authors are more readily available in European train stations than in the United States. An African writer we know whose book sold just over four thousand copies in the United States, sold 10,000 copies in The Netherlands and 30,000 copies in Norway, countries with much smaller populations. A book of literary short stories that sells five thousand copies in the United States, has a first printing of 15,000 copies in its Japanese translation.

This is embarrassing, isn't it? It is especially embarrassing at a time when, as a country, as a culture, and as individuals, for moral and economic and our own cultural reasons we need urgently to be aware of and sensitive to other cultures. We need, in other words, to be culturally literate. If we are not persuaded by moral arguments in favor of broadening our understanding of other cultures and ourselves, of joyfully championing and encouraging diversity of cultures and expression, of expressing our need for peace through our appreciation of other people and countries... if the moral arguments don't persuade us, increasing international economic interdependence soon will.

2

OUR INTENTION in compiling this anthology, our sixth *Graywolf Annual*, is to suggest the great range and variety there is among modern "Stories from the Rest of the World," and to offer a stimulus for further exploration of contemporary world literature. We were and are dismayed at our own unfamiliarity with writing by non-Western authors, and hope to share these few of our discoveries with readers of the *Graywolf Annual*.

Reading an anthology of short stories by contemporary writers from another culture is the next best thing to traveling there. The reader's intimate encounter with the people and concerns of a place offers tremendous challenges and an opportunity for a fresh view of his or her own culture.

As in other forms of friendship, in order to understand and appreciate, one must meet the other a bit more than halfway. Setting aside expectations of plot, character development, a clear "beginning, middle, and end," or of what we regard as conventions of literary style is of great benefit to opening oneself to the stories included here.

We must open ourselves to a different aesthetic model. If we perceive and are put off by stiffness in the plot, a static character, or clumsy language, we may entirely miss the music of these tales. Punjabi stories, for instance, are often carefully patterned after certain tales of the *Pancha tantra*, the Buddhist *Jatakas*, the *Hitaupadesh*, or other religious texts. They often carry a subtext as well, a background with which almost all literary communication is understood to be in dialogue, of the Punjabi struggle for independence. If we judge these stories strictly on our own terms, we may easily miss their beauty and their point. It can be a struggle for a reader unaccustomed to reading the myths and stories of another culture to overcome resistance and predisposition, but once the struggle is made, one is rewarded by a broadened awareness of the human condition, and an enormous respect for the magnificent courage and scope of so many international writers.

The strongest impression received from a reading of dozens of books of contemporary short stories in translation is a sense of how politically alert are the writers, the characters, and the cultures in which the action takes place. Most characters are keenly aware of their social station and sensitive to the political implications of their actions; the writers seem to have a political purpose in the writing of the story; and many of the stories seem to be written against a background, hidden to those of us who are "travelers," of social, historical, or cultural struggle.

"The Veteran," written in French by the eminent Congolese writer Henri Lopes, is included in this anthology in part because it is so typical of so many stories in non-Western cultures. Lopes makes use of his knowledge of politics (he has been prime minister of his country), and his story is openly and defiantly political. There is almost no "development" of character and plot, at least in the way Westerners usually understand it, but Lopes's conviction and energy for reform are evident. We sense in reading this story many aspects of African society: the interplay of the tribal and governmental loyalties; sensitivity to differences in social station; an ever-present caution about what one says and does, for one's actions and words are so often understood *politically* that one must constantly be alert to political trouble; a sense of overwhelming bureaucracy, its insistent involvement in everyday affairs and its irrelevance to the old culture of the nation; a sense that the individual sometimes has little control over his or her destiny. These themes are common in Arab and African stories; these stories can be judged by how grandly their political vision is expressed, by how well they have achieved their didactic purpose.

These are stories that *matter*, that do real work in the real world. They are not to be assessed in the same way we judge Literature written by authors who claim no political purpose. It is interesting, though, that after reading many sensitive political stories by non-Western writers the reader begins to see stories by certain American writers in an entirely new way. How is it that the African reader might interpret the stories of Raymond Carver?

For an American reader, born into a culture that places little value on art and artists, it is comforting to know that stories can carry such political and social weight.

3

THE STORIES included in this brief anthology were selected after reading through dozens of books of short stories published in all manner and forms. We limited ourselves to stories published in the 1980s, and though we at first intended to publish a broader survey of stories, we ended by concentrating our selection primarily on Asian, Arabic, and African short stories (with a fine Estonian story thrown in for good measure).

After a short while, we realized we were on something of a journey ourselves, hunting for treasures that were often exceedingly difficult to find. In order to find books of stories by non-American and non-European writers, we used every trick of interlibrary loan that we knew. Many editions were compiled by cultural ministries, who commissioned translations of their writers and produced books for international conferences. We found some books that carried no indication of who had published them.

We have often thought of translators as the unsung heroes of literature. Some of the translations included in this anthology, however, are haphazard, at best; despite some temptation to "improve" them, we finally thought it best to publish the stories mostly as we found them. The roughness, the foreignness, is part of the adventure of travel.

THE EDITOR of this anthology would like to thank the members of the Graywolf staff for their assistance in reading stories for this collection, and especially Katy Roberts, whose research was invaluable.

SCOTT WALKER
June, 1989

THE GRAYWOLF ANNUAL SIX

Stories from the Rest of the World

1 9 8 9

THE SILENT TRADERS

by Yūko Tsushima

Yūko Tsushima, born in 1947, is the daughter of
the Japanese novelist Osamu Dazai. She published
her first short story in 1969 and has published
twelve collections of stories in Japan. "The Silent
Traders" was awarded the 1983 Kawabata Prize.

Translated from the Japanese
by Geraldine Harcourt

T HERE was a cat in the wood. Not such an odd thing, really:
wildcats, pumas, and lions all come from the same family and even
a tabby shouldn't be out of place. But the sight was unsettling.
What was the creature doing there? When I say 'wood,' I'm talking
about Rikugien, an Edo-period landscape garden in my neighbourhood. Perhaps 'wood' isn't quite the right word, but the old
park's trees – relics of the past amid the city's modern buildings –
are so overgrown that the pathways skirting its walls are dark and
forbidding even by day. It does give the impression of a wood;
there's no other word for it. And the cat, I should explain, didn't
look wild. It was just a kitten, two or three months old, white with
black patches. It didn't look at all ferocious – in fact it was a dear
little thing. There was nothing to fear. And yet I was taken aback,
and I tensed as the kitten bristled and glared in my direction.

The kitten was hiding in a thicket beside the pond, where my

ten-year-old daughter was the first to spot it. By the time I'd made
out the elusive shape and exclaimed 'Oh, you're right!' she was off
calling at the top of her voice: 'There's another! And here's one
over here!' My other child, a boy of five, was still hunting for the
first kitten, and as his sister went on making one discovery after
another he stamped his feet and wailed 'Where? Where is it!' His
sister beckoned him to bend down and showed him triumphantly
where to find the first cat. Several passers-by, hearing my daughter's shouts, had also been drawn into the search. There were
many strollers in the park that Sunday evening. The cats were
everywhere, each concealed in its own clump of bushes. Their
eyes followed people's feet on the gravelled walk, and at the
slightest move toward a hiding place the cat would scamper away.
Looking down from an adult's height it was hard enough to detect
them at all, let alone keep count, and this gave the impression of
great numbers.

I could hear my younger child crying. He had disappeared
while my back was turned. As I looked wildly around, my daughter pointed him out with a chuckle: 'See where he's got to!' There
he was, huddled tearfully in the spot where the first kitten had
been. He'd burst in eagerly, but succeeded only in driving away
the kitten and trapping himself in the thicket.

'What do you think you're doing? It'll never let *you* catch it.'
Squatting down, my daughter was calling through the bushes.
'Come on out, silly!'

His sister's tone of amusement was no help to the boy at all. He
was terrified in his cobwebbed cage of low-hanging branches
where no light penetrated.

'That's no use. You go in and fetch him out.' I gave her shoulder
a push.

'He got himself in,' she grumbled, 'so why can't he get out?' All
the same, she set about searching for an opening. Crouching, I
watched the boy through the thick foliage and waited for her to
reach him.

'How'd he ever get in there? He's really stuck,' she muttered as
she circled the bushes uncertainly, but a moment later she'd

broken through to him, forcing a way with both hands.

When they rejoined me, they had dead leaves and twigs snagged all over them.

After an attempt of her own to pick one up, my daughter understood that life in the park had made these tiny kittens quicker than ordinary strays and too wary to let anyone pet them. Explaining this to her brother, she looked to me for agreement. 'They were born here, weren't they? They belong here, don't they? Then I wonder if their mother's here too?'

The children scanned the surrounding trees once again.

'She may be,' I said, 'but she'd stay out of sight, wouldn't she? Only the kittens wander about in the open. Their mother's got more sense. I'll bet she's up that tree or somewhere like that where nobody can get at her. She's probably watching us right now.'

I cast an eye at the treetops as I spoke – and the thought of the unseen mother cat gave me an uncomfortable feeling. Whether these were alley cats that had moved into the park or discarded pets that had survived and bred, they could go on multiplying in the wood – which at night was empty of people – and be perfectly at home.

IT IS exactly twenty-five years since my mother came to live near Rikugien with her three children, of which I, at ten, was the youngest. She told us the park's history, and not long after our arrival we went inside to see the garden. In spite of its being on our doorstep we quickly lost interest, however, since the grounds were surrounded by a six-foot brick wall with a single gate on the far side from our house. A Japanese garden was not much fun for children anyway, and we never went again as a family. I was reminded that we lived near a park, though, because of the many birds – the blue magpies, Eastern turtledoves, and tits – that I would see on the rooftops and in trees. And in summer I'd hear the singing of evening cicadas. To a city child like me, evening cicadas and blue magpies were a novelty.

I visited Rikugien with several classmates when we were about to leave elementary school, and someone hit on the idea of making a kind of time capsule. We'd leave it buried for ten years – or was it twenty? I've also forgotten what we wrote on the piece of paper that we stuffed into a small bottle and buried at the foot of a pine on the highest ground in the garden. I expect it's still there as I haven't heard of it since, and now whenever I'm in Rikugien I keep an eye out for the landmark, but I'm only guessing. We were confident of knowing exactly where to look in years to come, and if I can remember that so clearly it's puzzling that I can't recognize the tree. I'm not about to dig any holes to check, however – not with my own children watching. The friends who left this senti- mental reminder were soon to part, bound for different schools. Since then, of course, we've ceased to think of one another, and I'm not so sure now that the bottle episode ever happened.

The following February my brother (who was close to my own age) died quite suddenly of pneumonia. Then in April my sister went to college and, not wanting to be left out, I pursued her new interests myself: I listened to jazz, went to movies, and was friendly toward college and high school students of the opposite sex. An older girl introduced me to a boy from senior high and we made up a foursome for an outing to the park – the only time I got all dressed up for Rikugien. I was no beauty, though, nor the popular type, and while the others were having fun I stayed stiff and awkward, and was bored. I would have liked to be as genu- inely impressed as they were, viewing the landscape garden for the first time, but I couldn't work up an interest after seeing the trees over the brick wall every day. By that time we'd been in the district for three years, and the name 'Rikugien' brought to mind not the tidy, sunlit lawns seen by visitors, but the dark tangles along the walls.

My desire for friends of the opposite sex was short-lived. Boys couldn't provide what I wanted, and what boys wanted had noth- ing to do with me.

While I was in high school, one day our ancient spitz died. The house remained without a dog for a while, until mother was finally prompted to replace him when my sister's marriage, soon after her graduation, left just the two of us in an unprotected home. She found someone who let her have a terrier puppy. She bought a brush and comb and began rearing the pup with the best of care, explaining that it came from a clever hunting breed. As it grew, however, it failed to display the expected intelligence and still behaved like a puppy after six months; and besides, it was timid. What it did have was energy as, yapping shrilly, it frisked about the house all day long. It may have been useless but it was a funny little fellow. Its presence made all the difference to me in my intense boredom at home. After my brother's death, my mother (a widow since I was a baby) passed her days as if at a wake. We saw each other only at mealtimes, and then we seldom spoke. In high school a fondness for the movies was about the worst I could have been accused of, but Mother had no patience with such frivolity and would snap angrily at me from time to time. 'I'm leaving home as soon as I turn eighteen,' I'd retort. I meant it, too.

It was at that time that we had the very sociable dog. I suppose I'd spoiled it as a puppy, for now it was always wanting to be let in, and when I slid open the glass door it would bounce like a rubber ball right into my arms and lick my face and hands ecstatically.

Mother, however, was dissatisfied. She'd had enough of the barking; it got on her nerves. Then came a day when the dog was missing. I thought it must have got out of the yard. Two or three days passed and it didn't return – it hadn't the wit to find the way home once it had strayed. I wondered if I should contact the pound. Concern finally drove me to break our usual silence and ask Mother: 'About the dog... ' 'Oh, the dog?' she replied. 'I threw it over the wall of Rikugien the other day.'

I was shocked – I'd never heard of disposing of a dog like that. I wasn't able to protest, though. I didn't rush out to comb the park, either. She could have had it destroyed, yet instead she'd taken it to the foot of the brick wall, lifted it in her arms, and heaved it over. It wasn't large, only about a foot long, and thus not too much of a handful even for Mother.

Finding itself tossed into the wood, the dog wouldn't have crept quietly into hiding. It must have raced through the area barking furiously, only to be caught at once by the caretaker. Would the next stop be the pound? But there seemed to me just a chance that it hadn't turned out that way. I could imagine the wood by daylight, more or less: there'd be a lot of birds and insects, and little else. The pond would be inhabited by a few carp, turtles, and catfish. But what transformations took place at night? As I didn't dare stay beyond closing time to see for myself, I wondered if anyone could tell of a night spent in the park till the gates opened in the morning. There might be goings-on that by day would be unimaginable. Mightn't a dog entering that world live on, not as a tiny terrier, but as something else?

I had to be thankful that the dog's fate left that much to the imagination.

From then on I turned my back on Rikugien more firmly than ever. I was afraid of the deep wood, so out of keeping with the city: it was the domain of the dog abandoned by my mother.

In due course I left home, a little later than I'd promised. After a good many more years I moved back to Mother's neighbourhood – back to the vicinity of the park – with a little daughter and a baby. Like my own mother, I was one who couldn't give my children the experience of a father. That remained the one thing I regretted.

Living in a cramped apartment, I now appreciated the Rikugien wood for its greenery and open spaces. I began to take the children there occasionally. Several times, too, we released pet turtles or goldfish into the pond. Many nearby families who'd run out of room for aquarium creatures in their overcrowded apartments would slip them into the pond to spend the rest of their lives at liberty.

Rocks rose from the water here and there, and each was studded with turtles sunning themselves. They couldn't have bred naturally in such numbers. They must have been the tiny turtles sold at fairground stalls and pet shops, grown up without a care in the world. More of them lined the water's edge at one's feet. No doubt there were other animals on the increase – goldfish, loaches, and the like. Multi-storeyed apartment buildings were going up around the wood in quick succession, and more living things were brought down from their rooms each year. Cats were one animal I'd overlooked, though. If tossing out turtles was common practice, there was no reason why cats shouldn't be dumped here, and dogs too. No type of pet could be ruled out. But to become established in any numbers they'd have to escape the caretaker's notice and hold their own against the wood's other hardy inhabitants. Thus there'd be a limit to survivors: cats and reptiles, I'd say.

Once I knew about the cat population, I remembered the dog my mother had thrown away, and I also remembered my old fear of the wood. I couldn't help wondering how the cats got by from day to day.

Perhaps they relied on food left behind by visitors – but all of the park's litter baskets were fitted with mesh covers to keep out the crows, whose numbers were also growing. For all their nimbleness, even cats would have trouble picking out the scraps. Lizards and mice were edible enough. But on the other side of the wall lay the city and its garbage. After dark, the cats would go out foraging on the streets.

Then, too, there was the row of apartment towers along one side of the wood, facing the main road. All had balconies that overlooked the park. The climb would be quick work for a cat, and if its favourite food were left outside a door it would soon come back regularly. Something told me there must be people who put out food: there'd be elderly tenants and women living alone. Even children. Children captivated by a secret friendship with a cat.

I don't find such a relationship odd – perhaps because it occurs so often in fairy stories. But to make it worth their while the apartment children would have to receive something from the cat; otherwise they wouldn't keep it up. There are tales of mountain men and villagers who traded a year's haul of linden bark for a gallon and a half of rice in hard cakes. No villager could deal openly with the lone mountain men; so great was their fear of each other, in fact, that they avoided coming face to face. Yet when a bargain was struck, it could not have been done more skillfully. The trading was over in a flash, before either man had time to catch sight of the other or hear his voice. I think everyone wishes privately that bargains could be made like that. Though there would always be the fear of attack, or discovery by one's own side.

Supposing it were my own children: what could they be getting in return? They'd have no use for a year's stock of linden bark. Toys, then, or cakes. I'm sure they want all sorts of things, but not a means of support like linden bark. What, then? Something not readily available to them; something the cat has in abundance and to spare.

The children leave food on the balcony. And in return the cat provides them with a father. How's that for a bargain? Once a year, male cats procreate; in other words, they become fathers. They become father ad nauseam. But these fathers don't care how many children they have – they don't even notice that they are fathers. Yet the existence of offspring makes them so. Fathers who don't know their own children. Among humans, it seems there's an understanding that a man only becomes a father when he recognises the child as his own; but that's a very narrow view. Why do we allow the male to divide children arbitrarily into two kinds, recognised and unrecognised? Wouldn't it be enough for the child to choose a father when necessary from among suitable males? If the children decide that the tom that climbs up to their balcony is their father, it shouldn't cause him any inconvenience. A father looks in on two of his children from the balcony every night. The two human children faithfully leave out food to make it so. He comes late, when they are fast asleep, and they never see him or hear his cries. It's enough that they know in the morning that he's been. In their dreams, the children are hugged to their cat-father's breast.

We'd seen the children's human father six months earlier, and together we'd gone to a transport museum they wanted to visit. This came about only after many appeals from me. If the man who was their father was alive and well on this earth, I wanted the children to know what he looked like. To me, the man was unforgettable: I was once preoccupied with him, obsessed with the desire to be where he was; nothing had changed when I tried having a child, and I'd had the second with him cursing me. To the children, however, especially the younger one, he was a mere shadow in a photograph that never moved or spoke. As the younger child turned three, then four, I couldn't help being aware of that fact. This was the same state that I'd known myself, for my own father had died. If he had been dead it couldn't have been helped. But as long as he was alive I wanted them to have a memory of their father as a living, breathing person whose eyes moved, whose mouth moved and spoke.

On the day, he was an hour late for our appointment. The long wait in a coffee shop had made the children tired and cross, but when they saw the man a shy silence came over them. 'Thanks for coming,' I said with a smile. I couldn't think what to say next. He asked 'Where to?' and stood to leave at once. He walked alone, while the children and I looked as though it was all the same to us whether he was there or not. On the train I still hadn't come up with anything to say. The children kept their distance from the man and stared nonchalantly out of the window. We got off the train like that, and again he walked ahead.

The transport museum had an actual bullet-train carriage, steam locomotives, aeroplanes, and giant panoramic layouts. I remembered enjoying a class trip there while at school myself. My children, too, dashed excitedly around the exhibits without a moment's pause for breath. It was 'Next I want to have a go on that train,' 'Now I want to work that model.' They must have had a good two hours of fun. In the meantime we lost sight of the man. Wherever he'd been, he showed up again when we'd finished our tour and arrived back at the entrance. 'What'll we do?' he asked, and I suggested giving the children a drink and sitting down somewhere. He nodded and went ahead to look for a place near the museum. The children were clinging to me as before. He entered a coffee shop that had a cake counter and I followed with them. We sat down, the three of us facing the man. Neither child showed the slightest inclination to sit beside him. They had orange drinks.

I was becoming desperate for something to say. And weren't there one or two things he'd like to ask me? Such as how the children had been lately. But to bring that up, unasked, might imply that I wanted him to watch with me as they grew. I'd only been able to ask for this meeting because I'd finally stopped feeling that way. Now it seemed we couldn't even exchange such polite remarks as 'They've grown' or 'I'm glad they're well' without arousing needless suspicions. It wasn't supposed to be like this, I thought in confusion, unable to say a word about the children. He was indeed their father, but not a father who watched over them. As far as he was concerned the only children he had were the two borne by his wife. Agreeing to see mine was simply a favour on his part, for which I could only be grateful.

If we couldn't discuss the children, there was literally nothing left to say. We didn't have the kind of memories we could reminisce over; I wished I could forget the things we'd done as if it had all been a dream, for it was the pain that we remembered. Inquiring after his family would be no better. His work seemed the safest subject, yet if I didn't want to stay in touch I had to think twice about this, too.

The man and I listened absently as the children entertained themselves.

On the way out the man bought a cake which he handed to the older child, and then he was gone. The children appeared relieved, and with the cake to look forward to they were eager to get home. Neither had held the man's hand or spoken to him. I wanted to tell them that there was still time to run after him and touch some part of his body, but of course they wouldn't have done it.

I don't know when there will be another opportunity for the children to see the man. They may never meet him again, or they may have a chance two or three years from now. I do know that the man and I will probably never be completely indifferent to each other. He's still on my mind in some obscure way. Yet there's no point in confirming this feeling in words. Silence is essential. As long as we maintain silence, and thus avoid trespassing, we leave open the possibility of resuming negotiations at any time.

I believe the system of bartering used by the mountain men and the villagers was called 'silent trade.' I am coming to understand that there was nothing extraordinary in striking such a silent bargain for survival. People trying to survive – myself, my mother, and my children, for example – can take some comfort in living beside a wood. We toss various things in there and tell ourselves that we haven't thrown them away, we've set them free in another world, and then we picture the unknown woodland to ourselves and shudder with fear or sigh fondly. Meanwhile the creatures multiplying there gaze stealthily at the human world outside; at least I've yet to hear of anything attacking from the wood.

Some sort of silent trade is taking place between the two sides. Perhaps my children really have begun dealings with a cat who lives in the wood.

TWO BEDTIME STORIES

by Mori Yōko

Mori Yōko was born in 1940 and began writing at the age of thirty-five. She once wrote that she "is a complete devotee of things Western, who, even as a child, never went to see a Japanese movie."

Translated from the Japanese
by Makoto Ueda

Be It Ever So Humble
Sasayakana kōfuku

IT WAS slightly past lunchtime in the restaurant. Most of the customers had finished eating and were now sitting cosily behind their cups of coffee.

Through the window facing the main street the leafless branches of a maple, the image of a tree on a Bernard Buffet canvas, pointed at a cloudy winter sky. Apparently there was wind outside, for its naked twigs shifted uncomfortably in the chill of the afternoon.

Inside the restaurant, however, it was warm and restful. No music flowed; only the chimes of teaspoons on china accompanied the low melody of female conversation. Vases of bright flowers stood around like colorful islands among aromatic currents of espresso.

For some time now, Akiko had been gazing at the bare branches outside the window. The casual onlooker might have guessed her to be absorbed in admiring the wintery view; but, in fact, her expression was molded not from admiration but from bewilderment.

"Now I've told you the reasons," Aono said to her, fiddling with an empty wine glass. "I'm sorry."

He raised his eyes and stole a glance at her.

I'll be perfectly all right without him, Akiko persuaded herself. Until two months ago, I didn't even know this man Aono existed. It didn't inconvenience or depress me then, not knowing him. So I'm simply going back to the way it used to be – that's all.

The way it used to be. The thought rushed in with a flood of insufferable anxiety. She flicked her eyes up at Aono. No, she could never go back to the way it used to be. How could she return to the deathly boredom of that daily routine?

"I'm going to die," she groaned.

"Stop it! Don't make jokes like that," Aono did not try to hide his irritation. "We had our agreement, didn't we?"

"I wasn't serious. I only wanted to see how it would sound when I said it."

Aono looked relieved. Akiko averted her eyes from him. He is not what I really need, she thought. All I need is something to take me away from the kitchen and the TV once in a while. Anything that forces me out of the stifling comforts of my home just for a couple of hours. It doesn't have to be Aono. Heck, there isn't a single reason why it should be him. Except that he was interested in me.

An ache gripped Akiko's chest whenever she wondered why she had agreed to follow this stranger who had accosted her at a supermarket. Aono was precisely the type of man who would accost a housewife with a yellow shopping basket on her arm. That was Akiko's first impression of him.

In truth Akiko's pride was hurt when it happened. The man's once white shirt showed grubby cuffs from under his suit, and his hair was mousy.

A mousy kind of man, she thought. However, when he said he would like to treat her to a cup of tea, she accepted the invitation almost automatically because she was ashamed of herself for having been spoken to by that kind of man. There were a number of other women shoppers around her.

If she turned him down, and if he still went on propositioning her, the two would surely attract attention. Her only thought was to leave the spot as soon as she could.

Because she accepted his proposition so readily – although she was boiling inside – the man seemed momentarily flustered. Looking as if he could not believe his ears, he followed Akiko toward the exit.

In the end, she went to bed with him on that same day. As to why she would have done anything of the sort, she had no logical explanation. It was probably related to the same impulse that had made her act as she had at the supermarket earlier.

In the coffee shop they entered the man looked uneasy, but unable to hide what he had in mind.

"Uh – ma'am – you'll, er – come with me, won't you?" he said falteringly, avoiding her eyes. "Won't you please?"

There was no reason why Akiko should go with him. Everything about him irritated and repelled her. She felt insulted by his attentions; she could not forgive him for assuming her to be so cheap.

She couldn't help noticing the suspicious glances being cast in her direction from tables nearby – from a couple of housewives of about her own age, and from several girls, probably office secretaries taking extra-long coffee breaks. The glances disturbed her, urged her into action and so she ended up whispering "All right" to the man.

Even at that point, Akiko had no doubt there would be a chance to free herself from him once they left the coffee shop. All she had to do was tell him she had changed her mind.

She stepped outside while the man was paying for their coffee. The sun was beginning to set. The evening glow over the metropolis was filtered by dust. A piece of plastic whirled by her in an eddy of wind that also carried with it the smell of sizzling beef from a nearby restaurant. Akiko wondered what she would prepare for dinner.

She thought of the small kitchen at home, of the lunch dishes left unwashed in the sink. She could even visualize the lipstick stain on the rim of her coffee cup above the dried coffee dregs.

As the last blur of the tired sunset struggled through the gritty haze the temperature seemed to plunge. Akiko shivered. At that instant she was struck by the desperate feeling that nothing mattered anymore. In that cozy home of hers was there anything she really cherished? She was overcome by a terrible sense of futility.

The man came out of the coffee shop. When he saw Akiko, he blinked a few times and forced out a grin. "I was afraid you might have left," he explained almost apologetically. Obviously he had expected her to be gone by now.

"Why a lady like you? I still can't believe it. I'm mystified." He kept shaking his head as they started to walk together.

Despite his thin shoulders, he had a pair of stout hands. At least, they looked clean. Akiko knew she would not recoil from those hands if they touched her. And, for that sole reason, she went to bed with this stranger, who said he was a salesman.

She had not expected any fireworks in bed. And she was right. Aono was clumsy, and his palms were oddly warm. The elastic in his black socks was worn and they hung limply on his ankles. Afterwards he muttered that he might be short of money to pay the hotel and with an embarrassed look accepted two thousand yen from Akiko.

"Well, then . . . ," Aono stammered as they were about to part. It was at that moment that Akiko clearly saw that he had been taken unawares by the turn of events just as much as she, and had been just as scared. Her tenseness dissipated. For the first time she felt some warmth, something akin to a tender affection, beginning to rise within her.

"Shall we meet again?" she suggested.

Aono's eyes opened wide. Then a smile appeared and spread over his face. There was a touch of boyishness in his expression.

"How?" he asked.

"Like today," Akiko answered softly. "That is, by accident."

They parted in front of the railway station. The sun was long gone. The wind of early winter chilled the gloom.

Akiko, however, had a comfortable refuge. After the bleakness of their clandestine lovemaking, it was a pleasant thought to know a husband and home awaited her no matter how small and humble that home was. She even saw herself as a happy woman.

DESPITE her promise to Aono that day, Akiko was distressed over the prospect of his reappearing at the supermarket. As she looked back, what she had done seemed incredibly imprudent. She tried to think of it all as an accident. For the next three days, she did not go to the supermarket.

On the fourth day she went there to do her shopping, deliberately choosing a time different from the usual. To her dismay, she found herself restlessly scanning around as soon as she had set foot inside the store. Aono was not there. She felt relieved, yet somehow let down. From the following day, she began going to the supermarket at her usual time – the time she had met Aono.

As days passed with no sight of him, her sense of relief gradually turned to disappointment; she felt as a woman who had been jilted by her lover after a one-night stand, her relationship cut short before anything worthwhile had developed.

On the ninth day, Aono showed up. He was standing behind a pillar near the cashier, looking as if he were trying to hide himself. As she walked toward him, Akiko knew her face was breaking into a blissful smile and was irritated with herself.

"What a coincidence!" he said.

"It certainly is," she responded, her eyes instantly reconfirming the sad memory of a thin-shouldered, shabby-looking man.

As anticipated, Akiko once more went to bed with him and, also as she had anticipated, she was once again disappointed. As before, he took two thousand yen from her – a transaction that was to be repeated in their subsequent meetings.

As they parted, Akiko felt a relief that swelled from the bottom of her heart. She resolved never to see him again. When she arrived back home she was so happy that she hopped around the rooms, lightly touching every piece of furniture; the cushions, the sofa, the drapery – everything looked fresh. When her husband came home, she was tempted to jump at him like a dog and lick his face all over. Of course she didn't, but in comparison with the frigid-looking hotel room she had entered with that wretched man, her home was a paradise. I must love my husband more than ever, she thought. I must protect my home more than ever! She experienced an attachment to her husband and home as never before.

Inexplicably, she continued to see Aono. He came to the supermarket once every five days or so, and whenever Akiko pondered on the continuing affair she felt sick at heart. But she also knew she would be crushed with despair if Aono should stop appearing.

She did not even know whether he was married. She did not care. Aono as a person did not interest her in the least. Sometimes she would wonder why it was him she had responded to. A number of men had accosted her before. Most were definitely more handsome and better dressed than Aono; some of them youthful college students in blue jeans. But she had never entertained any idea of responding to a single one of them. With pride, she had turned her back on them, assuring herself she was not that kind of woman.

After she became acquainted with Aono, too, some men who saw her in the crowded street or at the railway station tried to invite her out for a cup of tea. Each time she resolutely shook her head and ignored the invitation.

As time passed, Akiko's irritation grew whenever she found Aono leaning against his usual pillar in the supermarket. He seemed completely without shame.

But she became even more upset when he did not show up and several more days would pass, in which she would repeatedly curse him for having such a nerve. Yet, as soon as he reappeared she felt her body grow heavy with a gentle numbness; her heart quietly surrendered to affection, and she was ready to follow him as if manipulated by invisible strings. Not once did Aono wear a new pair of socks.

"WELL, I'll be going then," mumbled Aono from the other side of the table.

Akiko stared at his face, which looked more ashy than ever. I've learnt almost nothing about him, she thought. Have I ever tried to study that pale face seriously?

Aono reached for the bill and started to rise from his chair. At that instant Akiko felt a choking sensation in her throat.

"What will become of me?" The words spilled from her mouth involuntarily.

Startled, the man's mouth dropped open. "What? What do you mean?"

"It's intolerable," she stuttered. "Without any discussion, you go ahead and announce that we'd better not meet again. I won't accept it!"

Behind him, the leafless branches were now swaying wildly. The lead sky had dropped into an even gloomier mood. At any moment, it would begin to snow or sleet.

"I suggested it because I thought it would be better for both of us." Aono meekly looked down.

"Don't decide by yourself what's best for us. How can you tell what's on my mind?"

Like a man pained by the cold, he contracted his body further.

"There'll be nothing left for me – absolutely nothing," Akiko groaned in a small, pathetic voice. "If you walk out on me like this, and if I can't see you again, there'll be nothing left for me."

She was well aware of the utter falsity of all this, for she still had a husband and home. The lie, however, expressed precisely her feelings at that instant; reason had been confused, the circumstances out of her control by the thought that this man was about to desert her.

"You say there'll be nothing left, but..." Aono searched desperately for the words to a way out. "You say there's nothing left, but you still have a husband, don't you?"

Her answer was ready without preparation. "It's because of you that I manage to get along with my husband. Because I have you, I can go on living in my house." Once again, truth and untruth became confused. Tears came to her eyes. "I'm not making any big demand. I'm not asking you to marry me. If you can keep seeing me as before – once every five days or so, even once every ten days – that's all I ask."

"You can say what you want, but . . . ," he paused, unconsciously crumpling the bill in his hand. "I don't think I can go on with it."

"Why not? Am I being unreasonable?"

The restaurant was now a sea of empty tables. Its lunch period ended at two o'clock and the shop was to be closed until five. It was a few minutes past two. Waiters were clearing away the last dishes.

"I feel uneasy," Aono looked around the room as if seeking help, "because I don't understand all this. I'm sure you're a good person, but . . . "

Suddenly it was as if Akiko had awakened from a spell; something freed itself inside her. Gone was the numb feeling she always had when she was with Aono. It was replaced by an unaccountable impulse to burst out laughing. Soundlessly she began to chuckle.

Dumbfounded, Aono stared at the giggling woman. His stupefied face was so funny that she laughed and laughed, until her eyes were brimming over with tears.

As she continued to laugh, though, she felt a coldness growing in her chest. Deep inside her, she sensed the opening of a dark abyss.

Aono rose hurriedly from his chair, an awkward twist on his face. "Well, I've got to go." He hovered for a second, his eyes still warily on Akiko. Her gaze was fixed, not on him, but on the barren branches outside the window. He turned and started to walk away. From behind, Akiko's low voice murmured something after him.

As soon as the man had disappeared from her sight, her face regained its normal composure.

A waiter came to tell her that the restaurant was closing for the afternoon. With a bright nod she stood up and walked toward the door, the subdued sound of her heels echoing through the empty room. This is the way it should be, she thought. What a relief! Good thing I was able to end the affair so easily. One little problem, and the man might have kept pestering me until I had a marital crisis. I wasn't in love with him anyway – I didn't even like him. Thank goodness he's gone, that's a load off my mind! Akiko opened the glass door. A cold wind, funneled up by the spiral stairway, blew right at her face. It swept away her sense of relief, and in its place left a devastating loneliness.

Just as she had feared, she was overwhelmed with the prospect of having nothing left, that the man had taken everything away with him. She felt abandoned by the entire human race.

With the greatest effort she climbed down the steel stairway, placing her feet with deliberate care. Her body seemed out of gear. Barely managing to steer herself, she at last stepped on the ground.

If she were to head for home right away, she would reach there at around three. She could visualize herself seated in her usual corner of the sofa with a cup of coffee. She could even see the automatic movement of her hand turning on the TV switch. No doubt she would gaze at the television screen as usual – with no enjoyment whatsoever.

Akiko started to walk aimlessly in the opposite direction from home. Several people brushed past her. One of them, a young woman, glared at her and said, "Watch where you're going!" Akiko was taken aback – had she been staggering?

The dark blanket of the sky was so low it seemed about to settle over the leafless branches. If it was going to be a snowy end to the afternoon Akiko wanted it to start right away. With her chin buried into the collar of her overcoat, she stopped at an intersection to wait for the traffic signal.

A number of other people were waiting there, some of the more impatient men already standing in the road. Because Akiko had no reason to hurry, she lingered on the sidewalk after the signal had turned green.

Then it happened.

"Won't you have a cup of tea with me?" A man's voice breathed closely in her ear. It was so close, indeed, that she could feel his warm breath on her neck.

Suppressing an impulse to jump back, she looked at the man. Her first impression of him was of the color gray. Perhaps it was because of his gray suit. The next instant, her eyes were on his hands.

"All right," she said with a faint nod.

By the time they had crossed the road, Akiko found herself intimately walking with him shoulder to shoulder.

Spring Storm
Haru no arashi

T H E S M A L L orange light on the lobby wall showed the elevator was still at the seventh floor. Natsuo's eyes were fixed on it.

From time to time her heart pounded furiously, so furiously that it seemed to begin skipping beats. For some time now she had been wild with excitement.

Intense joy is somewhat like pain, she thought. Or like a dizzy spell. Strangely, it was not unlike grief. The suffocating feeling in her chest was almost unbearable.

The elevator still had not moved from the seventh floor.

The emergency stairway was located alongside the outer walls of the building, completely exposed to the elements. Unfortunately for Natsuo, it was raining outside. There was a wind, too.

A spring storm. The words, perhaps romantic, well described the heavy, slanting rain, driven by a wind that had retained the rawness of winter. If Natsuo were to climb the stairs to the sixth floor, she would be soaked to the skin.

She took a cigarette from her handbag and lit it.

This is unusual for me, she thought. She had never smoked while waiting for the elevator. Indeed, she had not smoked anywhere while standing up.

Exhaling the smoke from the depths of her throat, she fell to thinking. I'll be experiencing all kinds of new things from now on, I've just come a big step up the ladder. No, not just one, I've jumped as many as ten steps in one leap. There were thirty-four rivals, and I beat them all.

All thirty-four people were well-experienced performers. There was a dancer with considerably more skill than she. Physically also the odds were against her: there were a sizable number of women with long, stylish legs and tight, shapely waists. One Eurasian woman had such alluring looks that everyone admired her. There were professional actresses currently active on the stage, too.

In spite of everything, Natsuo was the one selected for the role.

When the agency called to tell her the news, she at first thought she was being teased.

"You must be kidding me," she said, a little irritated. She had indeed taken it for a bad joke. "You can't trick me like this. I don't believe you."

"Let me ask you a question, then," responded the man who had been acting as her manager. In a teasing voice, he continued, "Were you just kidding when you auditioned for that musical?"

"Of course not!" she retorted. She had been quite serious and, although she would not admit it, she had wanted the role desperately. At the audition, she had done her very best.

"But I'm sure I didn't make it," she said to her manager. "At the interview, I blushed terribly."

Whenever she tried to express herself in front of other people, blood would rush to her face, turning it scarlet.

"You're a bashful person, aren't you?" one of her examiners had commented to her at the interview. His tone carried an objective observation rather than sympathetic inquiry.

"Do you think you're an introvert?" another examiner asked.

"I'm probably on the shy side," Natsuo answered, painfully aware that her earlobes had turned embarrassingly red and her palms were moist.

"The heroine of this drama," added the third examiner, "is a spirited woman with strong willpower. Do you know that?"

Natsuo had sensed the skepticism that was running through the panel of examiners. Without doubt she was going to fail the test, unless she did something right now. She looked up.

"It's true that I'm not very good at expressing myself, or speaking up for myself, in front of other people. But playing a dramatic role is something different. It's very different." She was getting desperate. "I'm very bashful about myself. But I'm perfectly all right when I play someone else."

If I am to express someone else's emotion, I have no reason to be shy, she confirmed to herself. I can calmly go about doing the job.

"Well, then, would you please play someone else?" the chief examiner said, with a nod toward the stage.

Natsuo retired to the wings of the stage and tried to calm herself. When she trotted out onto the stage and confidently faced them, she was no longer a timid, blushing woman.

It was impossible to guess, though, how the examiners appraised her performance. They showed little, if any, emotion. When the test was over there was a chorus of murmured "Thank yous." That was all.

Her manager was still speaking on the phone. "I don't know about the third-raters. But I can tell you that most good actors and actresses are introverted, naive, and always feeling nervous inside."

He then added, "If you don't believe me, why don't you go to the office of that production company and find out for yourself?"

Natsuo decided to do just that.

At the end of a dimly lit hallway, a small group of men and women were looking at a large blackboard. Most of the board was powdered with half-obliterated previous scribblings, but at the top was written the cast of the new musical, with the names of the actors and actresses selected for the roles.

Natsuo's name was second from the top. It was scrawled in a large, carefree hand. The name at the top was her co-star, a well-known actor in musicals.

Natsuo stood immobile for ten seconds or so, staring at her name on the blackboard. It was her own name, but she felt as if it belonged to someone else. Her eyes still fixed on the name, she moved a few steps backwards. Then she turned around and hurried out of the building. It never occurred to her to stop by the office and thank the staff.

Sheer joy hit her a little later.

It was raining, and there was wind, too. She had an umbrella with her, but she walked without opening it. Finally realizing the fact, she stopped to unfold the umbrella.

"I did it!" she cried aloud. That was the moment. An incomparable joy began to rise up inside her, like the bubbles crowding to exit from a champagne bottle; and not just joy, pain as well, accompanied by the flow and ebb of some new irritation. That was how she experienced her moment of victory.

When she came to, she found herself standing in the lobby of her apartment building. The first person she wanted to tell the news to was, naturally, her husband, Yūsuke.

The elevator seemed to be out of order. It was not moving at all. How long had she been waiting there? Ten minutes? A couple of minutes? Natsuo had no idea. Her senses had been numbed. A round clock on the wall showed 9:25. Natsuo gave up and walked away.

The emergency stairway that zigzagged upwards was quite steep and barely wide enough for one person, so Natsuo could not open her umbrella. She climbed up the stairs at a dash.

By the time she reached the sixth floor, her hair was dripping wet and, with no raincoat on, her dress, too, was heavy with rain.

But Natsuo was smiling. Drenched and panting, she was still beaming with an excess of happiness when she pushed the intercom buzzer of their apartment.

"Why are you grinning? You make me nervous," Yūsuke said as he let her in. "You're soaking wet, too."

"The elevator never came."

"Who would have considered using the emergency stairs in this rain!"

"This apartment is no good, with a stairway like that," Natsuo said with a grin. "Let's move to a better place."

"You talk as if that were something very simple." Yūsuke laughed wryly and tossed a terry robe to her.

"But it is simple."

"Where would we find the money?"

"Just be patient. We'll get the money very soon," Natsuo said cheerfully, taking off her wet clothes.

"You passed the audition, didn't you?" Yūsuke asked, staring intently at her face. "Didn't you?"

Natsuo stared back at him. He looked nervous, holding his breath and waiting for her answer.

"Natsuo, did you pass the audition?" As he asked again, his face collapsed, his shoulders fell. He looked utterly forlorn.

"How... ," she answered impulsively, "how could I have passed? I was just kidding."

Yūsuke frowned. "You failed?"

"I was competing with professionals, you know – actresses with real stage experience. How could I have beaten them?" Natsuo named several contending actresses.

"You didn't pass?" Yūsuke repeated, his frown deepening. "Answer me clearly, please. You still haven't told me whether you passed."

"What a mean person you are!" Natsuo stuttered. "You must have guessed by now, but you're forcing me to spell it out." Her eyes met his for a moment. "I didn't make it," she said, averting her eyes. "I failed with flying colors."

There was silence. Wiping her wet hair with a towel, Natsuo was aghast and mystified at her lie.

"No kidding?" said Yūsuke, starting to walk toward the kitchen. "I was in a state of shock for a minute, really."

"How come? Were you so sure I wouldn't make it?" Natsuo spoke to him from behind, her tone a test of his sincerity.

"You were competing with professionals." There was not a trace of consolation in his voice. "It couldn't be helped. You'll have another chance."

Although Yūsuke was showing sympathy, happiness hung in the air about him.

"You sound as if you were pleased to see me fail and lose my chance."

Combing her hair, Natsuo inspected her facial expression in the small mirror on the wall. You're a liar, she told her image. How are you going to unravel this mess you've got yourself into?

"How could I be happy to see you fail?" Yūsuke responded, placing a kettle on the gas range. His words carried with them the tarnish of guilt. "But, you know, it's not that great for you to get chosen for a major role all of a sudden."

"Why not?"

"Because you'd be a star. A big new star."

"You are being a bit too dramatic." Natsuo's voice sank low.

"When that happens, your husband would become like a Mr. Judy Garland. Asai Yūsuke would disappear completely, and in his place there would be just the husband of Midori Natsuo. I wouldn't like that."

"You're inventing problems for yourself," she said, "You are what you are. You are a script writer named Asai Yūsuke."

"A script writer who might soon be forced to write a musical."

"But hasn't that been your dream, to write a musical?" Natsuo's voice was tender. "Suppose, just suppose, that I make a successful debut as an actress in a musical. As soon as I become influential enough and people begin to listen to what I say, I'll let you write a script for a musical."

"Let you write, huh?" Yūsuke picked on Natsuo's phrasing. "If you talk like that even when you're making it up, I wonder how it'd be for real."

The kettle began to erupt steam. Yūsuke flicked off the flame, dropped instant coffee into two cups, and splashed in the hot water.

"Did you hear that story about Ingrid Bergman?" Yūsuke asked, his eyes looking into the distance. "Her third husband was a famous theatrical producer. A talented producer, too." Passing one of the cups to Natsuo, he continued. "One day Bergman asked her producer-husband, 'Why don't you ever try to get me a good play to act in?' He answered, 'Because you're a goose that lays golden eggs. Any play that features you is going to be a success. It will be a sellout for sure. For me, that's too easy.' " Yūsuke sipped the coffee slowly. Then, across the rising steam, he added, "I perfectly understand how he felt."

"Does this mean that I'll have to be a minor actress all my life?" Natsuo mused.

"Who knows? I may become famous one of these days," Yūsuke sighed. "Or maybe you first."

"And what would you do in the latter case?"

"Well," Yūsuke stared at the coffee. "If that happens, we'll get a divorce. That will be the best solution. Then, neither of us will be bothered by all the petty problems."

Natsuo walked toward the window. "Are you serious?" she asked.

"Yes." Yūsuke came and stood next to her. "That's the only way to handle the situation. That way, I'll be able to feel happy for you from the bottom of my heart."

"Can't a husband be happy for his wife's success?"

"Ingrid Bergman's second husband was Roberto Rosselini. Do you know the last words he said to her? He said, 'I'm tired of living as Mr. Ingrid Bergman.' Even Rosselini felt that way."

"You are not a Rosselini, nor I a Bergman."

"Our situation would be even worse."

From time to time, gusts of rain slapped at the window.

"When this spring storm is over, I expect the cherry blossoms will suddenly be bursting out," Yūsuke whispered.

"There'll be another storm in no time. The blossoms will be gone, and summer will be here." Brushing back her still-moist hair with her fingers, Natsuo turned and looked over the apartment she knew so well.

"You've been standing all this time. Aren't you getting tired?" her husband asked in a gentle voice. She shook her head.

"You're looking over the apartment as though it were for the first time," Yūsuke said, gazing at his wife's profile. "Or, is it for the last time?"

Startled by his last words, Natsuo impulsively reached into her handbag for a cigarette and put it in her mouth. Yūsuke produced a lighter from his pocket and lit it for her.

"Aren't you going to continue with your work this evening?" she asked.

"No. No more work tonight."

"What's the matter?"

"I can't concentrate when someone else is in the apartment. You know that, don't you?"

Natsuo nodded.

"Won't you sit down?" Yūsuke said.

"Why?"

"I have an uneasy feeling when you stand there and smoke like that."

Natsuo cast her eyes on the cigarette held between her fingers. "This is the second time today I've been smoking without sitting down." The words seemed to flow from her mouth at their own volition. His back towards her, Yūsuke was collecting some sheets of writing paper scattered on his desk.

"You passed the audition. Right?" he said. His voice was so low that the last word was almost inaudible.

"How did you know?"

"I knew it from the beginning."

"From the beginning?"

"From the moment you came in. You were shouting with your whole body – 'I've made it, I'm the winner!' You were trembling like a drenched cat, but your face was lit up like a Christmas tree."

Natsuo did not respond.

"The clearest evidence is the way you're smoking right now."

"Did you notice it?"

"Yes."

"Me, too. It first happened when I was waiting for the elevator down in the lobby. I was so impatient, I smoked a cigarette while standing. I've got the strangest feeling about myself."

"You feel like a celebrity?"

"I feel I've outreached myself."

"But the way you look now, it's not you."

"No, it's not me."

"You'd better not smoke standing up."

"Right. I won't do it again."

There was silence.

"You don't at all feel like congratulating me?" Natsuo asked.

Yūsuke did not answer.

"Somehow I knew it might be like this," Yūsuke continued. "I knew this moment was coming."

Now she knew why her joy had felt like pain, a pain almost indistinguishable from grief. Now she knew the source of the suffocating presence in her chest.

"That Rosselini, you know... " Yūsuke began again.

"Can't we drop the topic?"

"Please listen to me, dear. Rosselini was a jealous person and didn't want to see his wife working for any director other than himself. He would say to her, 'Don't get yourself involved in that play. It'll be a disaster.' One time, Bergman ignored the warning and took a part in a play. It was a big success. Rosselini was watching the stage from the wings. At the curtain call, Bergman glanced at him while bowing to the audience. Their eyes met. That instant, they both knew their love was over, with the thundering applause of the audience ringing in their ears... " Yūsuke paused, and then added, "I'll go and see your musical on the opening day."

Natsuo contemplated her husband's face from the wings of the room. He looked across.

Their eyes met.

WHAT SHOULD I DO?

by Chen Guokai

Chen Guokai, born in 1938, was an electrician before he wrote down "What Should I Do?", a popular story that had been widely circulated by word of
mouth. He was then invited to become a professional writer and has become well known as an
author of short stories.

*Translated from the Chinese
by Kenneth Jarrett*

I

TO THE GIRL that I was, life seemed a sunlit road strewn thick
with fresh flowers — smooth, pleasant, and beautiful.

Although I lost both my parents when I was young, I had a
wonderful aunt — my father's sister — who raised me all by herself.
She was an engineer in a research institute of chemical engineer-
ing, and a spinster. She had fallen in love as a college student but
the affair had ended in heartbreak. This killed her desire for
romance and kept her from ever marrying. After my parents
passed away, my aunt took meticulous care of me; her love for me
exceeded the love most mothers feel for their own daughters.

Probably because of my aunt's melancholy, I was not as fond of
singing and dancing as most other girls were. I liked quiet. I liked
to be alone, quietly reading a book. My aunt was a stern disciplin-
arian and paid close attention to my behavior. Once she sighed

and said, "Zijun, you're very beautiful. In fact, you're too beautiful
– it's a kind of affliction. You'll have to be especially careful in
life!" My aunt's advice summed up the lessons of her own life, but
these were lost on me. I thought that in our new society, flooded
with brilliant sunshine, the Party and Chairman Mao had arranged a happy future for my generation. What affliction could I
possibly have?

In a monotonous but pleasant way, our life passed peacefully
and quietly, like running mountain streams. My aunt often said
wistfully that "if it weren't for the Communist Party and
Chairman Mao, I don't know how we two weak women would get
by." My aunt's love for the Party and Chairman Mao was deep and
sincere. When I became old enough to understand, she often explained to me how without Chairman Mao we would not have a
new China or a happy life. Many years earlier, my frugal aunt had
used her hard-earned money to buy an expensive statue of
Chairman Mao carved in ivory. She had solemnly placed it on a
dark wooden table covered with red satin. At the foot of the statue
she placed a flower vase with gold ornamental engraving. Every
day after work my aunt would stop at a florist to buy some fresh
flowers, which she would reverently place in the vase beneath
Chairman Mao's statue. Then, each evening, under Chairman
Mao's benevolent gaze, we would happily study, work, chat, or
listen to fine music. I would often recite passionate poems by
Pushkin or He Jingzhi[1] for my aunt. Those days could hardly have
been more joyous.

In 1964 I completed an accelerated course at the university. I
had excellent grades and was assigned to be a technician in a machine factory. The following year I was sent to a large factory in
the provinces for in-service training. The person in charge of my
instruction there was a technician named Li Liwen. A brilliant student who had graduated two years earlier from Qinghua University, he had a personality that matched his name – slightly femi-

1. He Jingzhi (1924–   ), a well-known poet and playwright, and Vice-
Minister of Culture during this time.

nine.[2] He was good-looking, but I looked down on him to a certain extent because I felt he lacked masculinity. Whenever I encountered his bashful manner, I would stare at him, challenging him, until he became quite confounded. This gave me great pleasure. But on one occasion I got my just deserts. He was trying to plan a technical improvement, and I was helping him with the sketches. Out of carelessness I drew a machine axle incorrectly. Moreover, I failed to follow the normal procedure, which was to give the plans to him for checking, and instead handed them directly to a craftsman to begin work. Some time later Liwen came looking for me, axle in hand. His face was red with anger as he slammed the axle onto my desktop: "You did this! How idiotic!" Who would have thought a man like him could get so angry? I was dumbstruck. "This is design paper, you know, not a schoolboy's writing pad! Mistakes like this would be hard to make even with your eyes closed! Do you know how much material and work time have been wasted because of your drawing? This is alloyed steel bought with precious foreign currency, not a washing board or a fireplace poker!" With these words he launched a verbal barrage at me. I had never been dressed down by anyone like that before. I was so upset I began to cry, but he just continued to shout. My shame turned to anger, and I finally slapped the table. "I quit!" I covered my face and ran from the room. I was so angry I couldn't eat all day.

At sunset I was still sitting – feeling miserable – in the cool woods of the factory park by the river. As I sat gazing at the meandering stream, he quietly appeared at my side, his head lowered to look at me. He was obviously searching for something appropriate to say, but could not find it even after a long time.

Finally he muttered, "The Party branch secretary criticized me. I – I was wrong. I was rude to a comrade who had come to us from another factory. Will you forgive me?"

I did not answer.

2. The first character "li" in the given name Liwen means "beautiful." Although very common in women's names, it is rarely used for men.

"Please criticize me." After saying this he was quiet again for a long time. Then he placed a bag of something next to me and said, "I bought these fried dumplings at the mess hall. You haven't eaten, have you?"

My heart jumped, but I still didn't look directly at him. He just stood there dumbly. After a long time, he sighed and said, "You probably grew up in a city, so you don't realize how difficult it is to get that kind of imported steel. I was born and raised in a fishing village. During school vacations when I went home I'd go out fishing with my family. It was really hard work. You can't imagine how much fish and shrimp it takes to earn enough for one piece of alloyed steel. That's why I blew up."

I was deeply stirred by these words. It was as though I had touched a brilliant, glowing heart. My eyes were moist but I still said nothing.

He stood for a while, then quietly left.

Love can come to a young girl in many strange ways. My heart had become inexplicably tied to his by the sudden eruption of this quarrel. I studied hard under his guidance. Sometimes, in order to help me understand some technical problem, he would patiently repeat his explanations again and again. He often stayed busy deep into the night, and I would stay at his side. Under the bright light of lamps, surrounded by the sound of machines in the quiet night, our hearts grew closer and closer. Finally, late one blissful evening, as we were returning from the factory, the smell of machine oil still clinging to our bodies, I timidly offered him my young girl's heart.

I will never forget our parting that evening. We sat in the factory park until late at night. Then for the first time I experienced his awkward embrace; the deep impression of his kiss was left on my lips.

2

FOR SOMEONE in love for the first time, life becomes a source of excitement, anxiety, and restlessness. My sensitive aunt discovered that Cupid's arrow had already pierced my heart. But when she learned that my beloved lived so far away, she became deeply worried. "Do you understand him?" she asked. "Are you sure he truly and sincerely loves you?"

"I understand him as well as I understand myself," I answered.

"Don't be so naive about love," she sighed. "What's going to happen when you have to remain separated for a long time? Remember the old saying about 'too far away for the whip to reach the horse'? You'd be better off finding a good man nearby. It'd save you lots of worry, and let your aunt relax, too."

We could not agree on this point. But she was still very understanding and, except for an occasional sigh, did nothing else to interfere. She just watched anxiously as our love continued to grow.

We communicated our love through letters. I sent one about every three days. Anyone passionately in love hopes to get love letters that are long and detailed, every word revealing a burning, restless heart. But often his letters seemed perfunctory. One time he even requested that we write less frequently because he was busy working on an important technical innovation. I was very angry. But I forgave him when I remembered how often he neglected even food and sleep for his work. Not long afterward he sent me a newspaper with his photograph and a description of his achievements. I was indescribably happy and immediately sent him a telegram to congratulate him. The newspaper story also made my aunt feel better about him.

Our romance was at its peak when the Cultural Revolution began. I became drawn in by the tempestuous struggle around me. I watched thousands of young people march through the streets, as though drunk or mad, holding aloft Chairman Mao's little red book. I felt a profound admiration for it all. I believed this great movement to spread Mao Zedong Thought would have tremendous significance in combating and preventing revisionism. But it was quickly obvious that reality was falling far short of my ideals. The movement, begun as a political debate, soon entered its violent stage. I was sickened by the indiscriminate beatings, arrests, public humiliations, and ransacking of people's homes. I felt great sympathy for the cadres, workers, and technicians who were turned overnight into "monsters" of every description. The high hopes I had begun with were being torn to pieces. I was terrified that some disaster might befall my aunt, who was an intellectual from a merchant background. But luckily the political torrents did not reach our doorstep. My aunt was a cautious person. She had worked many years as a technician, had no quarrel with the world or anyone in it, and hence was spared personal attack at the onset of the Cultural Revolution. She exhorted me repeatedly to be cautious – to give people leeway in whatever I did and to avoid involvements in conflicts.

I felt confused that people's behavior in the movement was so at odds with Chairman Mao's original spirit, and I therefore stood aside from the struggles. I became, in fact, one of the "disinterested faction." But I remained deeply worried about what was happening to my distant lover. I waited for his letters even more anxiously than before. From them I learned that he was still buried in his studies and technical experimentation, but that his spirit was in torment because his work could not proceed as smoothly and effectively as before. He wrote about the vehement criticism of a veteran Party branch secretary who had always helped him carry out technical innovations, about the dissolution of his factory's worker-technician-cadre committee,[3] and about promising innovations turning into pipe dreams. He felt unhappy and hurt, but there was nothing he could do. I could well understand the agitated and despondent feelings of a dedicated technician unable to pursue the work he loved, and I was worried that this despondency would cause him to do something foolish. It seemed to me that only passionate love might relieve his anguish. I decided to move our marriage date earlier so that his agitated spirit could find peace in my warm embrace.

3. This was the name for many local administrative bodies before the Cultural Revolution; they were later replaced by Revolutionary Committees consisting of soldiers, "revolutionary" cadres, and members of the "revolutionary masses."

It was in 1967, when the call to "Attack with Words and Defend with Weapons"[4] rang out and "all-out civil war" began, that my lover came to my side. To the accompaniment of gunfire and bomb explosions in the city, we raised our wine glasses and with blushing faces drank a wedding toast in front of my aunt, relatives, and friends.

Around this time, factories were grinding to a halt. Factory Party organizations found themselves with no way to exercise authority amid the bewildering but intense struggle between opposing factions. Our honeymoon months passed in this unusual environment. Marriage caused ourfeelings for each other to reach new heights, but I discovered that when my husband was quiet, his face would take on a pensive or blank expression. He was thinking about his factory and the technical innovations he had left unfinished. At times, even when he was in my tender embrace, he seemed preoccupied with telling me how his technical innovations would help production leap ahead. That's when I realized that a woman can never command 100 percent of her husband's heart when his love for his work and factory are so deep.

After Chairman Mao issued the call for revolutionary unity, the battles in the factories gradually ceased. When my husband's factory sent him a letter asking him to return, I was already pregnant.

It is always sad when a loving couple has to separate. On the evening before his departure we were awake the whole night; our impassioned conversation was like an endlessly flowing stream, like a thread that couldn't be broken. We talked excitedly about our future home and child, and thought long and hard about a good name for the child. Finally we decided on Li Sijun.[5]

The next day, I faced the freezing wind and saw my husband off at the railroad station. After his train disappeared from sight, I suddenly felt my heart tighten. Tears rolled down my face like pearls off a broken string.

4. This slogan introduced the violent phase of the Cultural Revolution.
5. "Jun" is the same character used in Zijun's name; "si" is "thinking of." Hence the child's name suggests "thinking of Zijun."

3

I PASSED several quiet months enjoying the kicking of my unborn child. But less than two months before the baby was due, an ominous shadow suddenly fell over me.

Soon after Liwen returned to his factory, he sent me a letter that contained unusually strong language. His equipment had been totally destroyed. Seeing the fruits of several years' work go completely to ruin brought him to tears. His letter expressed intense anger at the outrageous behavior of the "rebels" who were holding the factory. Immediately I began to worry about his own situation.

A month later I received a letter whose language was even stronger. It told how, in the name of purifying the class ranks, the people in charge of the factory had launched an all-out reign of terror against the workers and staff. Some of his good colleagues had been subjected to persecution for no good reason at all. What especially upset him was that the chief mechanical engineer, a founding elder of the factory and a man he respected immensely, had been persecuted to death on groundless charges. His letter expressed his anger: "I cannot keep quiet. I must protest – "

This alarmed me. During those years, to protest injustice was to invite trouble. I hurriedly wrote him a letter asking him to come for a visit, which would place him outside the political maelstrom. After mailing the letter I counted the days on my fingers, but no response came within the expected period of time. Overcome with anxiety, I sent a telegram. But again there was no answer. An ominous feeling came over me. At the same time, a check of the class ranks was begun in my own neighborhood. The frightening atmosphere of arbitrary arrests and beatings increased my feeling of terror. I decided to set out in search of my missing husband.

Two days and nights on the train brought me to my husband's factory. I was received there by the arrogant and domineering head of a special investigation team. He listened to my story and then said, icily, "Your husband is an out-and-out counterrevolutionary. He attacked the rebels, attacked Red political power, and even had the audacity to seek scandalous material against us. He has already met a shameless end. You want to see him? Fine." He went to a room to get something – a bag – that he threw at me. "But you've come a bit too late," he said. "This counterrevolutionary has already committed suicide to escape punishment. He will remain forever an enemy of the people – "

My head throbbed. Losing the last ounce of strength in my body, I fainted. When I regained consciousness I found that I had been dragged into a deserted corridor. No tears would come, for I could not believe that my husband was a counterrevolutionary. I did not believe that a technician who had devoted all his intelligence and strength to socialist construction could be a counterrevolutionary. I just trudged away, holding to my breast the last possessions of my husband. When I reached the railroad station, I peered at those long tracks extending into the dark night. It occurred to me to end my grief by destroying myself. But just as I started walking dumbly toward the rails, the child inside me stirred. This made me realize I had a responsibility toward a little life. I halted, in a daze.

When I got home, completely exhausted, I was dealt another staggering blow. I knocked at my aunt's door and, when the door opened, found to my surprise a strange man standing before me. Inside was a completely different set of furniture and household articles. I was dumbstruck. For a long time I couldn't say a word.

"Your aunt was a suspected enemy agent. She died in the 'cow shed'[6] and has already been cremated. This apartment belongs to our research institute and has been assigned to me." The door slammed shut.

I raced to my aunt's office only to learn that on the third day after I had left home, my aunt had been accused of being a secret enemy agent and put into the "cow shed." This preposterous conclusion had been reached on the basis of her unhappy love affair long ago. While studying in the university, she had fallen in love with a young man of a wealthy family. Although she offered her young

6. Popular term for confinement areas for errant cadres and intellectuals.

girl's love to him, he suddenly abandoned her and married a young woman from another rich family. He ridiculed and insulted my aunt to her face. Afterward, this rich man's son became a member of the CC Clique and a leading figure in the Sino-American Cooperation Institute.[7] At Liberation he fled to Taiwan. Who would have thought that this bitter episode from the past could become "evidence" that my aunt was an enemy agent? Even more absurdly, it was claimed that the reason my aunt had never married was that she wished to remain faithful to this kingpin spy. My aunt had not been in good health. She had been suffering from serious heart trouble and had not been able to stand this mental and physical torture. After a few days in the "cow shed," she had died of a heart attack.

Dragging legs of lead, I left my aunt's institute and headed numbly toward my factory. When I entered my office I saw that my desk had been moved to a corner and was being used as a table for water bottles and miscellaneous items. The head of the design section forced a smile. "Zijun," he said, "the factory investigation office has notified us that because of your relationship to your aunt and husband, you are no longer suitable for work in this section. They also said that you must report to them as soon as you return." The section head looked at my blank expression and added compassionately, "Zijun, you're an honest person. I sympathize deeply. I did ask the investigation office to allow you to remain in the design section while you clear up your problem, but – " He threw up his hands, shrugged his shoulders, and heaved a long sigh. "Cheer up, Zijun. And take care of yourself. Go on living – don't do anything foolish."

I went to the investigation office and was given a routine

7. The CC Clique was a powerful faction in the KMT (Nationalist Party) in the 1930s and 1940s. Composed mainly of bankers and businessmen, it was named after its leaders, Chen Lifu and Chen Guofu. The Sino-American Cooperation Organization was a KMT military advisory group based in Chongqing (Chungking).

talking-to by one of its members. Then they handed me a small label with the words, "Counterrevolutionary Family Member," which I was to fasten to my blouse as a mark of my status. I was told to join the factory labor brigade to sweep the streets. They also ordered that every evening I write a confession of the crimes I had committed in the past and a report on my thinking that day. Seeing the small, black "Counterrevolutionary Family Member" sign on my chest and feeling the long bamboo broom in my hand, I realized that I had fallen among the dregs of society. My heart was broken – all hope was gone!

Carrying a child about to be born, I quietly swept the streets. I did not cry. I did not even grieve. The blows that had rained upon me had already deadened my emotions. I moved the broom as if I were a robot; it was only the occasional movement of the child that reminded me I was a living thing.

Dusk fell. I was permitted to put down my broom and return home. But where was home? The laws of the state clearly provided that the rights and interests of workers should be protected and that the property and personal freedom of every citizen should be safeguarded. But where was the law now? Where was truth? Where were the people's democratic rights? Who was it that had deprived me – an innocent, ordinary citizen – of my human rights?

I walked aimlessly through the streets. Close to midnight I found myself at the riverbank. Looking at the murmuring, flowing river, I thought that here my body and soul could rest forever.

The cool, salty night breeze gently caressed my hair. The dense evening fog lightly moistened my benumbed skin. I took my last glimpse of the world and with my unborn child threw myself into the river. . . .

4

I DON'T know how I regained consciousness. I opened my eyes in a daze. When I saw the white curtains, the white bedsheets, and the medical equipment in the room, I realized I was in a hospital for the living and not in the dragon palace at the bottom of the sea.[8]

At my side, watching me wake up, was a kindly woman doctor in a white hospital jacket. She sighed and pointed toward the foot of the bed. "This comrade saved you," she said. "He's watched over you the entire night."

I looked up wearily. Sitting on a long wooden bench – asleep – was a young man about my age. At first the stranger's image was vague, but it gradually became clear to me. It seemed I had seen that face somewhere before. Suddenly I remembered. It was my high school classmate Liu Yimin! I was stunned.

Liu was the son of a dock worker. His shoulders were broad, his face dark and square. He had inherited the rough personality of a dockhand; he preferred action to words. In our class he had been known as an arbiter of truth and justice because he liked to stand up to unfairness and was always willing to help his weaker classmates. I had heard that he became a factory worker after graduation, but I had long since forgotten him. Who would have imagined the strange coincidence that would bring us together again in this hospital ward, he in the role of my savior?

From his point of view, perhaps, saving a person from death was a noble act. But from my point of view, there was not the slightest cause for gratitude. In fact I felt bitter: I had already surrendered my sorrow and despair to the endlessly flowing water, and he had only salvaged my suffering and grief and returned them to me. His intentions had been good, but he should have minded his own business!

He awoke and saw that I had regained consciousness. "Comrade Xue Zijun," he cried happily. "You're awake!"

I closed my eyes wearily and did not answer. My former classmate's voice caused me to recall those student days, so filled with ideals and aspirations. What wonderful times those were! A romantic spirit had filled the air; singing, laughter, and gaiety

8. In Chinese legend, four dragons – controlling rainfall, storms, lightning, and thunder – reign over the sea.

were everywhere. On quiet evenings we innocent and naive girls would sit outside on the smooth green lawn of the school yard to gaze at the brilliant full moon and count the twinkling stars. Our thoughts seemed to grow wings that carried us across the heavens toward the shining Big Dipper. With vivid imagery we would describe our shining futures in impassioned tones. We all wanted to become like stars, eternally embedded in the vast heavens above our motherland, adding brilliance to our motherland's glorious face. I never imagined that in just a few years' time, the stars of our ideals would turn to scattered dust and that I myself would become an outcast.

I slowly opened my eyes, only to hear my classmate sigh and say, "This is not the way to deal with life."

Life – what was life? The reality before my eyes was like a black fog obscuring my vision; it blocked out the sunshine, cut off the green mountains, smothered my vitality, and cast a heavy, stifling shadow over my heart. I sighed weakly. "You're too meddlesome," I whispered. "You haven't saved me. All you've done is thrown me back into misery." My eyes were brimming with tears.

I heard the sound of footsteps. Two doctors, a man and a woman, appeared at my side. The man spoke. "The two of you must go home," he said. "The patient will be all right." His voice was warm but firm.

"Please let her stay in the hospital a few days. She's weak and – " My former classmate was speaking, but the male doctor interrupted.

"No," he said. "The hospital leadership wants her to leave immediately. They say the hospital is not a place for seeking refuge from class struggle."

Confused though I was, and though my body was as limp as a worn-out sponge, this remark felt like a needle piercing my heart. I strained to get out of bed and began walking toward the door. When I reached the door I almost fell. Liu Yimin supported me as we left the hospital. He called a pedicab and asked, "Where do you live? I'll see you home."

Where was home? "Just take me back where you found me," I answered. "I have no home."

A peculiar expression came over his face. After a moment of silence he said, "Mm – you'd better spend a few days resting at my house!" He helped me into the pedicab.

And so, without ever intending it, I ended up in his home. It was a wooden building on a secluded lane; his apartment was only about a hundred square feet. He told me that both his parents had passed away and that he lived alone. Then I learned that he was a maintenance electrician in one of the city's chemical factories. He said that the previous night, as he was cycling along the riverfront after work, he had suddenly seen someone fall into the river. He had jumped in to save the person. He had no idea the person he was saving was his former classmate until he had brought me to the hospital.

He briefly asked me about a few things, then went to prepare some food. Later he went out again and came back with a kindly looking old woman. "This is my aunt," he told me. "She's in charge of the neighborhood street association.[9]

If you have any problems, just ask her. She lives next door." With this he picked up his simple bedroll and headed for his factory. Only after he left did I notice the money, rice coupons, and other ration tickets that he had left on the table top. With them was a simple note explaining that they were for my use.

What happened that day had been complicated enough for a play. But, completely exhausted both physically and mentally, I was in no condition to ponder its meaning. When Liu and his aunt had left, I closed the door and, still muddle-headed, fell asleep.

I was awakened by an intensely agonizing pain and was taken immediately to an obstetrics hospital. My child was entering the world prematurely. When I looked into the little eyes, as clear as crystal, of this poor child who was fatherless from the moment it

9. Neighborhood street associations mediate disputes, monitor local opinion, and help to enforce public order and security.

joined the world, my maternal instinct returned. For this child I would stay alive no matter what!

5

MY RELATIONSHIP with Yimin was rather strange.

He came to visit after the child was born, and I could see that he really liked children. He held the child and began asking about its father. This led me to give him, for the first time, a detailed and tearful account of my misfortunes.

"Your husband really had guts," he said when it was over.

There was a long silence. Then he sighed and said, "These days bad people rule the roost and good people take it on the chin. At first I was all for the Cultural Revolution too. But later the blood and tears of so many old cadres and ordinary citizens helped me to see things more clearly." He was quiet for a while, then continued, "Seems like somebody's manipulating this movement. People wave the banner of the Party and Chairman Mao but in fact are blackening the name of the Party and Chairman Mao."

I had never tried to figure out the complicated background of this round of political struggle. I was only an ordinary person; what concerned me was how my child would survive. I was already at the end of my rope, with nowhere to turn. Suicide counted as "counterrevolutionary behavior" then, and unsuccessful suicide called for return to one's work unit for mass criticism. When the hospital notified my factory that I had jumped into the river, the factory investigation section – probably because they were still capable of a touch of mercy – did not try to trace my whereabouts or drag me back for criticism. All they did was discharge me. Thus I had no work, no relatives, and no home. For the moment, the only person I could depend on was this high school classmate. My fate and that of my child were in his hands. All he had to say was "please leave," and my child and I would be beggars in the streets. He had saved me out of the goodness of his heart, but he certainly had no obligation to support us.

We sat quietly, without speaking to each other. I felt like a prisoner in the dock, waiting to be sentenced.

Seeming to guess what I was thinking, he decided to speak. His voice was soft but very determined: "Don't worry. You can live here until you find work. Until then, I will cover expenses for you and your child."

Unable to control myself, I began to weep.

"Don't be too sad," he comforted. "The day will come when the black clouds pass and the sun comes out again."

To tell the truth, I felt quite unhappy becoming a heavy burden to a strange man. But what other choice did I have?

Why was this young man, neither well paid nor married, willing to make such a generous sacrifice for an orphan and widow he did not really know? Was it from deep, well-considered sympathy or just the emotional impulse of someone acting bravely for the sake of justice? Didn't he know that giving refuge to someone wearing the label "Counterrevolutionary Family Member" could be a heavy burden politically, emotionally, and materially? After a long silence, with tears in my eyes and my voice shaking, I asked, "Why do you want a person like me to stay here?"

"Why?" He was speechless. After thinking a while he finally said, "You ask me why, but I can't really say. Your question reminds me of a story, though." There was another silence before he began.

"When my father was alive, he told me this story many times. Once he was sick. One of the dockyard manager's regulations said that if a permanent dock worker was absent from work because of illness for more than three days, he would be fired. On the fourth day, when the boss was calling the name roster, someone answered my father's name and went off to work. This person even gave the money he earned to my father for medical expenses, until my father was healthy and able to go back to work. It was one of my father's co-workers, a night shift dock worker. In order to help my father stay alive, he did two shifts of coolie labor every day for ten days. This, I think, is our workers' class . . . our class feeling. It was just in this hand-in-hand, shoulder-to-shoulder way that the workers in the old society managed to get by." When he reached this point his rough face took on a dark expression. "I feel sure you're an innocent victim," he concluded.

From the plain words of this ordinary worker, I could see that the morality of the older generation of the proletariat had been passed down. Now, when evil influences were causing members of the same class to trample on each other indiscriminately, this dock worker's son suddenly appeared. He was like a glittering star rising over my gloomy spirit, giving me courage, letting me see light.

Thus began our very unusual relationship. We were neither relatives nor friends, but he still bore all expenses for me and my child. Each month on payday he came without fail to give me money. His salary was not high. He kept only $15 a month for himself; the rest he gave to me. He lived in the singles' dormitory at the factory. On Sundays he would come to visit me and my child. I ate sparingly and spent frugally, but I often prepared a nice meal on Sundays for my "benefactor." He would never eat it, though – he told me to give the food to the child. I asked him to put aside his dirty clothes until Sundays so that I could wash them, but he only laughed and shook his head. He said his hands were used to work. He would never stay long but just played with the child a while and left. He gave us much but never wanted the slightest thing in return. Sometimes as I watched his sturdy silhouette hurrying away, I would become so sad that I would break down and cry.

In this unique way we passed two years' time. Each month when he brought my living allowance, he would quietly put it under the glass on the writing table. He never presented it to my face. I knew why he was so circumspect: he didn't want me to feel like a dependent. But each time after he left, as I took his hard-earned money from under the glass top and recalled that I was a "good-for-nothing," rejected by society, again I could not help weeping.

I don't know how I got through those two years. I once tried to find work because I wanted to be independent. But what work unit would take a "Counterrevolutionary Family Member"? All my efforts were in vain. I not only didn't find work, but also had to depend completely on Yimin's aunt, in her role as leader of the street association, to avoid being counted among the neighborhood's Five Black Categories[10] and suffering further political humiliation.

My child could already sing. He was clever like his father, and thoroughly lovable. He and Yimin were very fond of each other. As soon as Yimin arrived on Sundays, the boy would cling to him and beg him not to leave. One time the innocent child blurted out something like, "Uncle, don't go. Live together with Mommy." I was so embarrassed I had to run into the bedroom. "Don't talk nonsense," Yimin said to the boy, then picked up the child and carried him outside. I don't know why, but those chance words from my little boy became fixed in my mind as if carved there. They threw me into some confusion, but upon reflection I realized the idea was impossible. A person as good as Yimin deserved the most beautiful and happy love in the world, not a widow with an orphan.

Yimin never talked to me about his own life. It was only by accident that I learned his love life, too, had been unhappy. One day I encountered on the street another high school classmate who had been one of Yimin's better friends. He expressed deep sympathy for my plight. We talked and talked, eventually coming round to Yimin. He said Yimin had once been in love with a certain girl who was also our classmate. The two had become engaged but had postponed their marriage when the Cultural Revolution began because they were too busy being "rebels." After a while Yimin had withdrawn from the rebel committee, but his fiancee became one of the leaders of the rebel clique and then managed to squeeze into the ranks of the "chiefs" of her work unit. After this she had cast aside Yimin, a mere worker, to marry a "top leader" whose position was even higher than her own. As if all this were not enough, she then trumped up some charges that Yimin was politi-

10. In the Cultural Revolution, much of the populace was divided into good (red) and bad (black) categories.

cally unreliable and brought them to his factory. Luckily Yimin's class background was good and he had also been a "rebel soldier," so the factory left him alone. But the incident had broken Yimin's heart; he swore that he would never marry.

At this point my schoolmate lost his temper right there on the street. "A woman like that is a disgrace to humanity! A calamity! A beast! If I ever run into her again I'll beat her up on the spot!"

Yimin's behavior gave every indication that he indeed lacked a girlfriend. I inquired everywhere about various female classmates from our high school days, hoping that I could help him find a mate. But all my efforts failed. No one knew where some girls were; others were already married; and a few, I heard, had even become those frightening "model" individuals. It was most frustrating.

By now three years had passed. It was 1971. I had gradually noticed a slight change in Yimin's feelings. As before, he brought us money every month. And every Sunday he would visit, play with my child for a while, and leave. But he stopped being as stubborn as he had been. When I once noticed that his jacket had a small hole in it and asked him to take it off and let me mend it, he did not resist. He watched bashfully as I sewed. When I raised my head and our eyes met, he suddenly blushed and looked away. There is nothing more sensitive than a woman's intuition. Yimin's actions made me sense that something new might be entering our lives. My face also turned red.

I was very frugal with the monthly allowance Yimin gave me. Beyond the food necessary for my son's growth, for my own food I was able to make two meals from a piece of fermented bean curd and some pickled vegetable. In this way I managed to save a little money each month. After three years, I had accumulated a considerable sum. I thought that if Yimin were to marry or to have some urgent need for money, then I would be able to give it to him. Now and then I sounded out the idea of buying him a bit of new clothing, but he refused. Once, though, when I noticed that his socks were worn out, I secretly bought him a pair of nylon socks. The next Sunday, when I gave him the socks, he cheerfully put them on. This change gave me a new feeling; I felt I should begin to take care of his personal needs. Surreptitiously, I noted his height and shoulder measurements and set about making him some clothing. One Sunday I placed before him a beautiful polyester jacket that I had painstakingly tailored.

"Where did you get so much money?" he asked, dumbfounded.

I laughed. "It's all your money, you know; it wasn't stolen. Try it on. See if it fits." I helped him put on the jacket, and he did not refuse. His face turned as red as a beet as I fastened the buttons.

"Thank you, Zijun," he said softly.

"If you have to thank me for this, how will I ever thank you?" I asked uncomfortably. "We've known each other three years, and you're still so polite." I don't know why, but tears started running down my face. When Yimin saw this, he was suddenly moved to hold my hand. My heart began to beat wildly. But Yimin regained his composure in just a few seconds. He hugged and kissed the child and then went out the door. He had great self-control.

I found myself in love. I loved him, really and truly loved him. I would have gone through fire and water for him. Life's sufferings and hardships had not ruined my looks, but I was, after all, a mother. From the time I noticed the change in Yimin's feelings, my soul had been calling out, struggling. I didn't know how to control my emotions.

Late in September, on one of Yimin's paydays, it had been raining steadily. I felt sure he would not come. But at eight o'clock in the evening, after the child was asleep, someone suddenly knocked on the door. It was he. He stood in the doorway wearing a raincoat; outside, the rain was pouring down. I rushed to welcome him in. As he took off his raincoat he said, "There was a big meeting at the factory today. That's why I'm late." His face beamed with joy as he continued. "Let me tell you the great news — Lin Biao is finished!" Yimin was ecstatic. He pulled out a bottle of wine and said, "Tonight let's drink a farewell toast for those fascist bandits on their way to see Hitler!"

Throughout those months and years, I had been basically isolated from the world. This news came too suddenly for me; I didn't have time to think about its significance. But Yimin's wild joy was infectious. I rushed off to get wine glasses.

"The black clouds have passed! Soon the sky will be blue! We ordinary folk don't have to put up any more with the insults and persecution of Lin Biao and his fascist bandits! We can have a better life! Have some wine, Zijun!" He pushed a small wine glass, filled to the brim, in front of me. I was not a drinker but couldn't refuse when I saw how happy he was. In three years we had never sat face to face to drink a glass of wine or even to eat a meal. What a strange relationship!

I drank the wine and began to cough and choke; I coughed until my eyes watered. Yimin was looking at me intently. A passionate expression suddenly flickered across his face. "Zijun," he said in a soft voice, "you're really beautiful."

Embarrassed, I lowered my head; my whole face was ablaze. This was the first time in three years I had heard him make any comment about me. It was also the first time he expressed his love for me. Outside, the rain kept pouring down and the wind kept howling. Mother Nature seemed swept away in boisterous celebration. It was a moment that could have touched anyone's emotions. I lowered my head and waited for him to continue talking. But instead he calmed down; he changed the subject back to his feelings about the evil deeds of the bastard Lin Biao and his accomplices. He kept drinking as he talked, obviously needing to release his pent-up feelings, and his happiness, before me. He talked incessantly for over an hour saying more to me that night than he had in the past three years put together.

His mood affected me deeply. As I looked at the outline of his handsome lips and his clear bright eyes, I suddenly thought of my dead husband. No! Yimin was even stronger and more confident, his spirit even more generous. This worker had a kind of noble quality that commanded admiration and respect. He was the kind of person who, having set his goal, would fight for it against all difficulties. In the company of such a person, even the weak could gain strength.

I was losing myself in daydreams when he abruptly finished

talking. He glanced at his watch, stood up, and looked at me. "I'm going back to the factory," he said softly.

Startled back to the present, I looked at my watch. It was nine-thirty. The rain had not stopped. How I wanted him to stay! The words were on my lips and my face was red, but I couldn't say anything. I only muttered to myself, "It's raining so hard – "

He hesitated a moment, then went for his raincoat. Slowly, he put it on and walked towards the door.

A rush of hot blood surged to my head. I leaned against the door; passionate feelings had turned my entire face bright red. Looking at my toes, I continued speaking. "Yimin, don't – don't go. If – if you need me." My voice was so low it seemed as though only I could hear it.

There was a brief silence. Suddenly, I heard the sound of his raincoat being dropped in the corner. Then, a pair of powerful muscular arms tightly embraced me.

6

LIKE a dream, my life began a new chapter. Yimin and I were married.

Our married life was as harmonious and blissful as could be. To clear off the debts that were weighing on my conscience, I devoted myself entirely to Yimin.

When I was cleaning the apartment in preparation for our new married life, I thought that I would remove the wedding picture of Liwen and me from under the glass table top. I knew that some men resented such things. A man who marries a previously married woman will often expect her to rid herself of every trace of her former husband, including his memory. I knew Yimin was not that kind of a man, but to keep my old wedding picture on the new table was just too conspicuous. Yet Yimin discovered me removing the photograph and stopped me. "Leave it. He had great strength and courage. I respect him and hope you'll always remember him."

"The child is getting old enough to understand these things," I softly protested. "If he catches on, it could leave an emotional scar."

"Don't deceive the child," Yimin replied. "We should let him understand love and hate right from the start. If he knows his father was persecuted to death by Lin Biao and his gang, he'll love the Party and socialism even more. He'll grow up even faster. You can't feel love unless you've known hate."

I was moved to tears. Yimin gently caressed my shoulders. "Don't cry, Zijun. Lin Biao and his gang were taking too much from the Chinese people these past years. What we need isn't tears, but study and struggle. Get hold of yourself! You're a technical expert; you'll be able to use your knowledge in the future." He fell silent a moment, then continued. "We've all been muddling along these past few years. Now we can set up a home study program. You can be my teacher – teach me math and science." He smiled charmingly. "You were the class monitor in high school and a top student. Then you hit the books in college for a while. You're more than qualified to be my teacher, don't you think so, Teacher Zijun?"

Yimin's teasing made me smile through my tears.

Not long after our wedding, Yimin really did go out and find some math, physics, and chemistry textbooks. We sat under the bright light of a lamp, close together, reviewing old lessons. A teacher-student relationship grew in addition to our husband-wife relationship. My gallant husband, as he listened to my explanations with rapt attention, turned as docile as a child. Sometimes I helped him with innovations he was working on. Our family life was never dull. My son loved his stepfather, and Yimin's feelings for the child exceeded the love most fathers feel for their own sons.

After this marriage my child and I were no longer considered "Counterrevolutionary Family Members." I got temporary work in Yimin's factory. My monthly salary was only about $20, but this was enough to improve our family's economic situation greatly. I went off to work and came home together with Yimin, and we respected each other completely. I assumed the household work myself; all of my mental and physical efforts went to ensure that Yimin and the child were comfortable and happy.

Yimin headed a squad in his factory's electrical repair section. His work was outstanding; he was a model in the factory's campaign to "Learn From Daqing."[11] Yet I worried about him because of his overly straightforward nature and his habit of commenting on political events. At home he often spoke of Jiang Qing in contemptuous tones: "Can't that rotten actress be satisfied being a member of the Party's Central Committee? Does she have to go around shitting and pissing on the old generals' heads? She's the same ilk as Lin Biao. China's going to the dogs at the hands of leaders like these." I frequently advised him that ordinary people like us were better off not taking too much interest in politics. Unwilling to agree with me, he would only heave a sigh. "There is too much that is backward and feudal about China, and it is too deeply rooted," he would say.

The year 1975 arrived. As the Party's new policies began to take effect,[12] some of the changes affected our family. Yimin was promoted to section chief because of his outstanding work. One of his technical innovations, to which I too had made a contribution, was written up in the newspaper. Thanks to the concern of the factory's party committee, I was transferred from a temporary job to a permanent position with the technical group in a mechanical workshop. After the twists and turns of the past years, the brilliant sunshine of Mao Zedong Thought once again shone warmly on my body and lit up my home. I lamented only the fact that Liwen and my aunt had not lived to see this day. If they had been alive during this marvelous time, when the people's economy was ex-

11. Daqing, an oilfield in Heilongjiang Province, was a model for industry during the Cultural Revolution.
12. The Fourth National People's Congress (January 1975) restored Deng Xiaoping to high position and seemed to signal a policy shift toward domestic stabilization.

panding under the guidance of the Three-Point Directive,[13] just think how much they could have achieved!

That autumn I became pregnant. I was elated and excited; Yimin was also as happy as could be. He insisted on taking over all the household chores so that I could rest. He was the kind of man who could show great consideration for his wife. At his suggestion we decided to name our unborn child Liu Aijun.[14]

With the coming of winter, the north wind began to rise and the climate changed. The so-called "Counterattack the Rightist Tendency to Reverse Correct Verdicts" movement began.[15] Once again a political struggle engulfed the country. In many places factories stopped work. The interruption of rail service caused coal shortages at factories, leading to further delays. Production declined day by day, dashing the people's hopes and aspirations. The masses felt anxious and restive. In January 1976 the country suffered a severe blow with the death of Premier Zhou Enlai. Yet every day the newspapers continued to make oblique accusations against him. Deep sorrow and indignation weighed heavily in the people's hearts.

Yimin became very quiet during this period. I could easily sense the change. He often sat alone, lost in thought; at times he looked terribly depressed. I had a foreboding notion that something new was going to happen in our life. Sometimes I asked him what he was thinking about, but he couldn't explain. He would just use vehement language to comment on the political scene. Once, when he returned home very late, I asked him where he had been. Instead of answering my question directly, he pulled out some mimeographed material from his book bag and held it in front of

13. Deng Xiaoping's Three-Point Directive gave lip service to (1) the importance of class struggle but emphasized (2) economic development and (3) stability and unity.

14. "Aijun" – literally, "loves (Zi)jun."

15. This movement arrived in 1975 after Deng Xiaoping, the second most prominent target of the Cultural Revolution, returned to power. Radicals running the movement charged that "correct" political verdicts rendered during the Cultural Revolution should not be reversed.

me. I glanced at it and saw it was called "Collected Speeches of the Rightist Tendency to Reverse Correct Verdicts." It was a compilation, printed in Shanghai, of speeches by comrade Deng Xiaoping and other leading comrades of the State Council. "Look at this," Yimin said. "Uncle Deng's speech is the voice of the people, and the voice of the people will hold up under any criticism, any attack."

I read through without stopping this book of "lessons to learn from bad examples." It affected me deeply. The imposing image of an outspoken and frank old revolutionary, daring to speak out for the people, appeared before me, standing tall and upright like a monument. Without understanding everything, I could guess the nature of this struggle. As Yimin slept peacefully, I looked at his dashing eyebrows and handsome face. I silently pronounced a heartfelt wish – a wish that this struggle would not bring misfortune to my family. . . .

But, in the end, a terrible disaster befell me once again. On the third day after the Qingming Festival, a black automobile from the Municipal Public Security Bureau drove up to the factory. I received a phone call from a worker in the electrician's section saying that Yimin had been arrested. At once peals of thunder seemed to rock my head; the receiver in my hand hit the ground with a thud. As soon as I recovered I ran desperately toward the factory gate. There I saw my beloved husband – handcuffed – being led away by two policemen in white uniforms. He was walking erect and unafraid. Behind him followed a big crowd of spectators.

I ran toward him, tears falling like rain.

Yimin stood as stern as a stone carving when he saw me. His voice was firm. "Don't be afraid, Zijun. I haven't committed a crime. Take care of your health, and look after the child. I'll be back!"

I fainted. When I regained consciousness Yimin had already been taken away. Several workers who often spent time with Yimin had also been arrested.

Later I learned that Yimin had been arrested because he had

participated in memorial activities for Premier Zhou at the Qingming Festival. He had posted in the center of the city a large banner reading "Overthrow anyone who has the audacity to oppose our beloved Premier Zhou." He had also written a poem about Jiang Qing entitled "Denounce the White Bone Demon."[16] These activities had constituted "counterrevolutionary crimes" and were the reason he was now locked behind bars.

Back at home, I gazed at the memorial niche to Premier Zhou that my husband had set up. "Where are you, Premier?" I cried in my heart.

I had once again become a "Counterrevolutionary Family Member"!

7

IN OCTOBER 1976, an autumn breeze dispersed the sinister mist that lay across the land. The Party central leadership, led by Chairman Hua, smashed the Gang of Four with one stroke, rescuing the Party, the country, the people, and my family. Before then I don't know how many tears I cried, worrying day and night about whether my husband Yimin was dead or alive. But once the Gang of Four lost power, I calmed down. My years of misery and misfortune finally received an explanation. It became clear that the heinous Lin Biao and Gang of Four had been responsible for the profound difficulties of thousands of ordinary citizens like me. I further realized, for the first time, the far-reaching significance of the Cultural Revolution: although the destruction and interference of Lin Biao and the Gang of Four had exacted a heavy and painful price from the country, the Party, and the people, the Cultural Revolution had also profoundly instructed and tempered us. The great masses of people, while captive in a confusing and complicated struggle, had developed keen vision and could

16. White Bone Demon is a character in *Journey to the West* by Wu Cheng'en (c.1500–c.1582). The demon could change its outer appearance to disguise its wicked nature.

now discern truth, goodness, and beauty. A fearless young generation, like Yimin but millions strong, who would dare go through fire and water for the revolution, had been created.

I believed that my innocent husband would soon be released and allowed to return home. Looking at the portrait of Chairman Hua, I was moved to tears.

Those days, when the entire country was given over to revelry, I was going through the month of isolation customary after a woman gives birth. I asked someone to take two bottles of wine to my imprisoned Yimin. I knew he would be especially eager for wine.

I waited anxiously as a month passed, but Yimin did not come. So I went to the prison, carrying our one-month-old daughter with me.

There I saw my husband. He was much thinner. Several months of life behind bars had turned his face pale. Yet he was full of vigor and in high spirits. The first time Yimin saw his own flesh and blood he was as happy as a child; he stroked his daughter's head and played with her legs. "You were born at just the right time," he said to her, beaming with joy. "Your generation probably won't have to endure all the misery and difficulty of your parents' generation." Turning to me he asked, "Why didn't you bring Sijun? I really miss him."

"I didn't want any wound to be left in his young heart," I replied softly.

Yimin smiled. "You should let the child understand more! Let him know that during the rampage of Lin Biao and the Gang of Four, some organs of the proletarian dictatorship temporarily became tools to institute a dictatorship over the proletariat. This is a lesson that not only our generation but also our grandchildren and later generations must remember!"

I wished that he would not continue with this kind of talk. But he only smiled and said, "What are you afraid of? The Gang of Four have finished reading their lines. Now it's time for the people to speak." Then, in a darker tone, "I know this period has been difficult for you, Zijun."

What he said caused me to weep again.

After my hoping day and night for several months, one bright and beautiful sunny afternoon Yimin was proclaimed innocent, released from prison, and allowed to come home. When he reached home he embraced the two children and kissed them madly. Then he grabbed an empty bottle to go out for some wine. "Today I'm going to buy some good wine, prepare some good food, and enjoy a reunion meal," he said, cheerfully making his way down the stairs.

Little Aijun was sleeping. Just as I was preparing to wash the clothes that Yimin had brought back from prison, there was a knock on the door. How could he have returned so quickly? When I opened the door, I found a stranger standing there. He was wearing a pair of thick glasses. His hair was prematurely gray. His face was covered with terrifying scars, and his upper lip was horribly split. If I had come across such a face some quiet evening on the street, I think I would have screamed in terror.

"Who do you want?" I asked with fear in my heart.

The person looked directly at me. Suddenly, his face twitched violently. "Zijun," he said, in a strained and indistinct voice. "I'm Liwen!"

I felt as though a bolt of lightning had passed over my head, as though a peal of thunder had clapped in my heart. I was stunned. I leaned against the doorway. For a long time I couldn't say a word.

"Tell the truth, Liwen. Are you a person or a ghost?" I asked, trembling.

"What do you mean by that?" He was obviously confused and frightened.

"They said you committed suicide!" With chattering teeth, tears rolling down my cheeks, and a stammering voice, I briefly recounted the painful events that had transpired. His face resumed its frightening twitching. Having listened to my account, he gnashed his teeth and said, "They really did think I was dead. I'm a man who's clawed his way back from the netherworld. It all began when I exposed the criminal behavior of those murderers.

Then the beasts trumped up charges against me, saying I was a counterrevolutionary. I was thrown into the 'cow shed' and tortured. I was beaten with chains; ice water was poured down my nostrils; I was forced to lie down with my feet on a stool while heavy poles were placed across my unsupported legs; I was burned with an electric soldering iron until my face and body looked as they do now. For a whole day and night I was unconscious. They thought I was dead, so the bastards carried me to the railroad tracks near the factory to make it look like I'd committed suicide. A kindhearted worker saved me and secretly brought me to the hospital. But when the factory found out, they took me from the hospital and put me in prison. I was in prison for eight long years. They didn't let me out until a few days ago."

I looked at the many horrifying scars on my first husband's face. The poor man! The whole thing was heartbreaking! Think of the torment and suffering he must have endured all these years!

"But why didn't you ever write me a letter?" I cried.

He sighed. "Eight long years! They deprived me of freedom of speech and movement for eight years. How could I write a letter? I sent a telegram to your unit as soon as I got out of prison. I didn't get an answer, so I came in person. I asked and learned you had moved to this place." Tears flickered in his eyes; the scars on his excited face glowed; he looked like a person who, having been stranded on a deserted island for a long time, suddenly sees a rescue ship.

Memories of the loving couple we once had been, which were memories I had treasured over eight difficult years, now combined with my great joy at seeing my husband return from death and created a huge wave of emotion in me. My entire body felt soft and light, as if I were in a small boat that was thrashing about on the spray of the churning sea, then was hurled toward the mountaintops by a gigantic wave. How I wished I could immediately run up to Liwen and with both hands heal the scars that had been cruelly left on his face by Lin Biao and the Gang of Four. I would gently wash away the bloody wounds left on his heart and let his returned soul, which had suffered untold miseries, rest in my warm bosom.

"Eight years, Zijun! During those miserable years I never stopped thinking about you and the child. I might not have lived through it all if the two of you had not been in my thoughts. The heinous Lin Biao and Gang of Four broke up our family; but now, Chairman Hua and the central Party leadership are allowing this pitiable couple to be reunited!" He opened his arms excitedly. I could no longer control my emotions; choked with tears, I threw myself into his embrace.

The distinct sound of familiar footsteps came from the stairs. My other husband Yimin was back! The sound of his steps hit me with the force of an electric shock. I immediately struggled free from Liwen's embrace. My heart seemed to have been suddenly torn in two.

My God! What should I do?

S E E D S

by *Mahasveta Devi*

Mahasveta Devi, born in 1926, is a progressive
Bengali novelist and short story writer. She has had
more than 50 works published and lives in Calcutta.

Translated from Bengali
by the author

T HE LAND north of Kuruda and Hessadi villages is uneven,
dry and sunbaked. Grass does not grow there even after the rains.
There is an occasional cluster of cactus here and there, like snakes
about to strike but frozen still. Or some neem trees. In the middle
of this barren and arid stretch of land where not even a buffalo
grazes lies a tiny piece of low-lying land, hidden from the eyes by a
slightly raised embankment. It is about one-sixth of an acre of
land and visible only when one stands on the raised embankment.
It is only then that lush greenery of the land almost strikes one
hard in the eye. Incongruous, almost weird.

More weird is the tiny thatched shelter on a platform set on
wooden pegs. Totally out of place. Such shelters are usually made
for guarding the crops. But here on this land one sees only some
aloe plants with thorny, swordlike leaves. Even buffaloes avoid

them. Its fibres make good rope. But nobody here knows this use of aloe. It is just a wild plant to them.

But in the evening one sees probably the weirdest sight of them all. A human figure can be seen coming from the direction of the Kuruda village walking in long strides. When he comes nearer, one can see it's an old man, skin wrinkled with age, wearing a loin-cloth, a small bag made of cloth hanging from the waist. When he comes, he strikes on the aloe plants aimlessly with the stick in his hand. Then, after reaching the platform, he scrambles up a rick-ety ladder. Then he lights a *bidi* with flint and just sits there. After it is dark all around, he falls asleep. Every day.

Every day, back at the Kuruda village, his old wife loudly shouts and says things about him, which are not complimentary. His sons, their wives, their sons and daughters, are not too pleased at this rebuke, but they are helpless. Anyone intervenes, and he has had it. And who in this region is a match for Dhatua's mother in shouting and calling people names? In cases of dispute, her effi-cient and professional quarrelling faculties are eagerly sought af-ter by the disputing parties.

Everyone holds her in awe. During the Emergency, the police had come to the village in search of some villagers, one of whom was actually hiding in a cowshed when they came. Dhatua's mother screamed abuses at the police. "Come on, you bastards! Tear every hut apart and comb the village!" Her attitude and words were proof enough that the village was an "innocent" one. The police left. And then she started on the boy in hiding, "Rotoni, you are worse than an unsold she-goat. That you at-tacked the Rajput moneylender with a *tangi* was fine! Should have chopped his head off. But why come to the village? Go, scram! To the jungles in hiding."

Dhatua and Latua dare not tell their mother, "Don't abuse fa-ther so much." It would make her mad. So the father was every-thing and the mother nothing, was it? A king guarding his king-dom, that useless piece of land. And if he is bitten by a snake or snatched by a tiger, who would be widowed? The sons of their mother? If father died, who would look after the daily needs of the family? The sons? Could they, like their father, bluff the sarkar year after year into paying for paddy-seeds, fertilisers and price of bullocks for a land never cultivated? And plough and bullocks never purchased? And sell the fertiliser?

The sons keep silent. The mother after letting out the steam pulls at the *hookah* and mutters to herself, "He will be found dead one day and I won't be there to see him before he dies."

The sons know that their father is behaving strangely. Who keeps watch over aloe plants at night? But father has always been a very complex person and has done things which others would not dare think of. The Ganju people, in this region, skin dead animals and tan hides. Dulan had once killed with poison some buffaloes, belonging to the almighty Rajput landlord, the great Lachhman Singh, commanding ten shot-guns and rifles, cleverly, surreptitiously, right in the heart of Tamadi, Lachhman's village. No one suspected Dulan, a small fry, and Lachhman held his cousin Dwaitari, a rival, in suspicion. Thus an unending civil war between the two was unleashed.

It proves all over again that Dulan is different from the others. He knows how to do what. Busy in devising cunning schemes to make both ends meet, he had never had any time for his sons and grandchildren. The son's mother too is hardworking, courageous and quick to flare up. Not like the other women either.

The sons had never seen their parents sitting and chatting amiably. But father, whenever in a dilemma, made mother sit close beside him, offered her *hookah* and said ingratiatingly, "Say, Dhatua's mother! Do tell me what to do. You are the village adviser and counsellor. Even the police hold you in awe."

"What is the latest, crotchety one? Planning to bluff or rob someone?"

Once in a blue moon they behave like a loving couple, grown old together, friendly. But usually father does not have time for mother either. It makes mother angry and she threatens to leave for Tura, her father's village. It is an empty threat as all her people have died long ago. Father jeers at her and says, "Go at once! Your father has a big palace at Tura awaiting your pleasure."

No, Dhatua and Latua are no match for their parents. Shanichari, a village harridan, says, "Both of them are mad, your father doubly so. He gets land, he guards it, yet he does not sow paddy there!"

The land actually belongs to Lachhman Singh. Some time ago, the Sarvodaya workers had gone from door to door beseeching the landowners to gift away land to the landless. Shanichari used to say, "These ones are mad, too. They aim to soften the land-owners so that out of repentance they would give away some to the poor. If the maliks did that, why, I would cook rice twice a day, eat butter and drink milk."

But some of the maliks, just to spite their rivals, started giving away arid land in holdings. The Bhoodan did not help the poor. The maliks remained owners of big holdings. They cultivated wheat, paddy, *marwa*, mustard and lentils. Peanut was a new crop in the area, a cashcrop.

The Bhoodan served many purposes. For the Sarvodaya people it was a proof that they had succeeded in bringing a change of heart among the maliks of Palamau. This accomplished, they left for the Chambal ravines to work a change of heart among the dacoits. For the maliks, they got rid of wasteland and the receivers became their slaves, their goodwill with the administration was strengthened and, to crown it all, they were convinced that they were really and truly kind and generous.

Thus Lachhman gave the piece of land to Dulan. Dulan was not interested at all but Lachhman was adamant. "What! You lowcaste no good! Can't you see that I am doing this from a change of heart? I might change tomorrow."

"Hujur, you are my father and mother."

"If that is so, why are you grumbling? It's lowland. During the monsoon rains flow. Do work there and you would have bumper crops."

Dulan could have said that he would have to cover a mile of semi-desert to cultivate that small piece of land and it would not work. But he kept silent. He had gone to borrow some money, and came back a landowner burdened with a sense of dejection. The villagers consoled him, "Why take the malik seriously? He will forget all about it by tomorrow."

"What if he doesn't?"

"Leave it, don't cultivate. Everywhere the receivers are either selling or mortgaging the Bhoodan land. You too do the same."

The Pahan, the tribal priest, scolded Dulan. The villagers had lots of real problems. Dulan's problem was an insignificant one. Dulan felt even more dejected.

His wife said, "The old fox! You're just pretending. You're thinking of ways to make the land pay."

"That land? Pay?"

Shanichari said, "Why, Dhatua's mother? Let Dhatua's father go to the BDO at Tohri. The sarkar will give all the assistance, money, seeds, everything."

The land was ultimately in his possession after the registration was complete. A poor man, surrounded by rich Rajput maliks and moneylenders, and the mighty Brahmin priest Hanuman Misra of Tahar, he was desperate to retain his individuality and survive. With subversive cunningness and tenacity he managed somehow to fool the power-wielders and gain his end.

His wife and the villagers waited to see what Dulan would do. They greatly admired Dulan, the fighter, who managed to outwit the mighty with ingenuous and well-manoeuvred moves.

They knew all about the buffaloes, and never talked to Lachhman about Dulan. Once Dulan sold a pumpkin to Dwaitari and made both his mother and his wife pay him twice. On the day of the Chhat festival, he guarded the cart laden heavy with fruits and vegetables all the way from Lachhman's house to the banks of the river Kuruda, all the while shouting as if to drive away the birds and thus managed to steal some from the heap. Never did he share with others his thus-begotten gains. Yet they admired him. He did what all of them wanted to, but did not have the courage and self-confidence to do.

As soon as he received the *patta*, he touched Lachhman's knees and said humbly, "Malik Parwar! You've been so generous, but how shall I cultivate it? The BDO won't give me any help."

"Who says so?"

"I belong to a lowcaste, that's why."

"Sure you do, and you forget it, that's why you get kicked about. But since it's me giving you land, how come they won't help you? Who is the BDO?"

"A Kayastha, malik. He calls the Rajputs uneducated brutes and he uses his left hand to hold a cup of tea or a glass of water. Listens to the transistor all the time."

"Shame upon him, the left hand?"

"Yes, malik."

"Let me write him a letter. But listen, leave the land as it is. Don't sow anything on that land."

Dulan was perplexed but realized that it was useless to argue. He only said, "Malik!"

Lachhman's vakil drafted a letter on his behalf insisting upon payment of agricultural loan, fertiliser and seeds for Dulan for years to come. The BDO had already been warned by the SDO about the danger of incurring the wrath of either Lachhman Singh or Hanuman Misra. He agreed to everything, treated Dulan with marked courtesy and explained to him that he would receive seeds and fertiliser, and must secure plough and bullocks with a little advance and bring the bullocks to his office to claim the price.

Dulan told the Pahan, "This sarkar is very foolish. Who buys plough and bullocks on instalment? Lend me your bullocks please, so that I can take them and get paid."

Every alternate year Dulan took the same pair of bullocks and told the same story to the BDO. "The old ones died, hujur! What to do!" He took money for the bullocks, sold the fertiliser right at Tohri and carried the sack of paddy-seeds home. The first time his wife had said, "Why so much? How much is the land by measure?"

"You can't measure it."

"What do you mean?"

"It's for our empty stomachs. Can you measure hunger? Hunger knows no landmark."

"What shall you do with it?"

"Boil and husk it so that we can eat."

"Eat paddy-seeds? You will die."

"We ate mice during the famine and managed to survive. Die of eating paddy-seeds! No. If I do, I'll have the consolation of having tasted rice and I'll go to heaven."

After tasting rice, Dhatua's mother was convinced that she had never had a tastier meal. She boasted to the villagers that she was luckiest of all married women. Whose husband was clever enough to fool the sarkar and feed the wife with rice made from seed paddy?

The villagers shared her pride. No, the sarkar never took care of them. The BDO never gave assistance to the poor peasants. Their children were never allowed in the primary schools run by the sarkar. Lachhman and Dwaitari forced them to harvest either on a scanty meal or on twenty-five paise a day. Tension was mounting in the village because of this. In the adjacent blocks, the Dusads, Ganjus and the Dhobis were getting fifty paise a day. The villagers of Tohri block were keen to get the same, but they dared not raise their voices. They knew that if trouble broke over this, the SDO was sure to enter the village and arrest the trouble-makers. The sarkar belonged to the Lachhmans, Dwaitaris and Hanuman Misras. When a Dulan Ganju managed to cheat the same sarkar, why, hats off to him!

The land provided Dulan with six hundred rupees a year. Dulan slept at home. He and his wife shared one wooden platform in the veranda of their hut. An old he-goat was kept tethered under the platform, the goaty smell being a sure cure for asthma from which Dhatua's mother suffered. The hut was partitioned into two cubicles and Dulan's sons slept one in each with his wife and children. The inside of the hut was crammed with sacks of wheat or maize, firewood, earthen pitchers and what-not. The six hundred rupees were not enough for such a large family. Often Dulan and his sons went to the jungle to collect roots, fruits and tubers, to Tohri to carry luggage, to Hanuman Misra's extensive orchard to work on wages.

The Karan Dusad came to the village. A man of razorsharp intelligence, he used to work as a *khetmazdoor* for Lachhman. He fought with him for better wages for the *khetmazdoors*, was arrested and sent to jail. He came across political prisoners in Hazaribagh jail.

He was surprised to see that they did not hate him for being a Dusad and admired him for being a fighter. They were impressed to know that two hundred marginal peasants and *khetmazdoors*, without any political organisation to back them, had turned against the mighty Lachhman Singh and set fire to wheat-fields, driven desperate by naked exploitation. The boys told Karan that it was vital to organise a movement the way Karan did. Get organised and fight for your rights because you are being exploited. Fight from your base.

The political boys were often tortured by the prison authorities and went on hunger strikes. This led to merciless beatings, often ending in death. Yet they told Karan, "You're a fighter, you know. Did the correct thing. Do not ever change your ways."

Karan caught on. After being released, he told the villagers, "The conditions remain the same. Why wait till he forces us to rise against him and then take a bullet or go to prison? Let's unite and get organised. We'll talk with him, finalise our demands and ask the police to be present during the harvest. Our demands are very little. We the harijans and tribals of Tohri block want a twenty-five paise rise as others are getting in the other blocks. We won't get a decent wage in this godforsaken place ever. So let's launch a movement for twenty-five paise rise."

Dulan sent for Karan as soon as he heard of this. Cautious and wary by nature, he took Karan to the embankment surrounding his land for complete secrecy. Middle-aged, lean and small, Karan seemed to have become a changed person after leaving Hazaribagh jail. He startled Dulan by his opening sentence, "There's no such thing as caste-division and untouchability. The Brahmins and the wealthy have invented it."

"Ah, you are just repeating what the educated ones say. Listen to me carefully. The malik, the BDO and the SDO are drink-companions. Thick as thieves. Before you launch your movement go to the tribal office and the Harijan Seva Sangh at Tohri. Give them all the details. Take them with you to the *thana* when you go there to ask the police to be present during the harvest."

"Why, are we not enough?"

"No, you are not. Don't be a fool, Karan. The sarkar will help Lachhman. If the malik shoots at you, he will get away scotfree. But you're sure to be arrested if you just raise a stick. Ask Madan-lal of the Sangh to help you. He is a good man and the sarkar knows him."

Karan agreed, Madanlal had political influence too. The SDO and the daroga met Lachhman first, made a deal, and assured Madanlal later of all help.

Maize was harvested and carted away without any hitch. The mazdoors received their fifty paise wage as demanded. Karan Dusad became a hero overnight. The dreams came true. And Lachhman told Dulan, "Tomorrow, be on your patch of land in the evening. If you open your mouth about this, you'll be killed."

The next day, the SDO went to Ranchi and the daroga went away to faraway Burudiha to chase a dacoit. In the magical hour between sunset and night, Lachhman Singh raided the Dusad mohalla of Tamadi village with his caste brethren, the Rajput maliks. The huts blazed, the Dusads were trapped in the fire, mud walls were demolished. And, to Dulan, the new moon revealed a scene from the silent movies of yester-year. Lachhman was on horseback. An improvised platform placed upon two horses side by side carried more than one dead body. Ten gunmen of Lachhman followed the procession.

On gunpoint, Dulan was made to dig graves for Karan and his brother Bulaki. Lachhman supervised all the while chewing *paan*. When it was over he said, "One word from you, you son of a bitch, you'll join Karan Dusad. The jackals and wolves might dig up the grave. You will build a platform here and sleep on it to keep guard. Karan has started a fire and I, a Rajput, will see that other graves are dug." Dulan nodded his head in affirmation. Yes, why not?

The next day the police came to the village to make enquiries. But it came to nothing as Karan, according to police, was not present during the disturbances. None gave evidence against Lachhman. Reporters did not obtain enough material to justify "a true harijan story." A person in Lachhman's pay was arrested for arson. The SDO gave a meagre sum to the afflicted to build huts.

Dulan started staying on the raised platform in the nights. The sons, totally baffled, tried to dissuade him. But they failed to reach Dulan, who stared at them with bloodshot eyes. After a spell of uneasy silence, he raised his stick and growled, "Don't you dare talk to me, Dhatua. I'll kill you."

Dulan felt shaken, crushed and empty. He had been reared up in the belief that death, like birth, demanded set rituals. But Lachhman proved how outdated and futile those beliefs were. Two dead bodies on horseback and surely the Dusads of Tamadi knew all about it. Lachhman did not have to hide anything for he knew that the eyewitnesses would be too terrorised to open their mouths. They had read the warning in Lachhman's eyes, "Open your mouth and you are dead." It had happened before, it would happen again. It was necessary from time to time to set the night sky ablaze and screaming with the death-cries of the untouchables of this country just to drive the fact home that the Constitution of India, the Acts, Ordinances and Laws meant nothing really. A Rajput remained a Rajput, a Brahmin remained a Brahmin. The Brahmins, Rajputs, Kayasthas, Bhuinhars and Kurmis remained on the top of the ladder each in his own place and untouchables at the bottom. A Rajput, or a Brahmin, or a Bhuinhar, or a Yadava, or a Kurmi might be, in rare cases, as poor as, or even poorer than a harijan. But they would never be thrown in the fire because of their caste. During the mythical Khandavakanana fire the Agnideva had consumed some black-skinned forest-dwelling untouchables. His appetite for the flesh of the untouchables of this country had not been satiated till today.

The incident created a havoc in Dulan's psyche. Till now, all that he ever thought about was how to survive by devising what cunning. But now he himself seemed to have changed into a secret grave doomed to conceal two dead bodies. He could feel the dead putrefying, disintegrating, making him unclean. The secret entrusted by Lachhman became a deadweight weighing upon him and Dulan alone had to shoulder it. If he opened his mouth, the Dusad mohalla at Kuruda would burn too. Dulan became a pale, taciturn man.

Time passed. People were forced to keep silent about Karan and Bulaki. A newly opened railway line connected Burudiha and Phuljhori with Tohri. Certain Police Stations and SDOs were empowered to investigate into the incidents of tribal and harijan atrocities and take remedial steps. In the tribal and harijan village of Dhai, the panchayat dug a well. Thus this backward area, immersed in abysmal darkness, tried to reach the modern times.

It made Lachhman all the more powerful. He defied the agricultural labour wage-revision rules laid by the government and paid the *khetmazdoors* forty paise a day. He gifted a coiled cobra made of solid gold to the Shiva Linga worshipped by Hanuman Misra, a scooter to the BDO, a transistor to the daroga and took possession of half an acre of land belonging to Karan and Bulaki.

It was all in the order of the place, but suddenly, unexpectedly, there was a further agricultural labour minimum wage-revision and a new SDO was asked to implement it. The higher authorities suspected him to have left-leanings and, in order to test him, had asked him to implement the revised wage. Once he did so, his left-leanings would be proved and necessary steps against him would be taken. He came to take charge of the subdivision six weeks before the harvest. The authorities told him that the area was divided between rich uppercaste maliks holding all the land and the tribal and harijan *khetmazdoors* working for them. The latter had no faith in the former. Since the condition of the area was appalling, an enlightened and sympathetic officer was needed to effect the changes desired by the government.

The SDO suspected that it was the beginning of his end. He asked his father-in-law to look for an opening in a bank, readied himself to resign at the first chance and zealously, vigorously, went all out to see justice done. He told the *khetmazdoors* that they were entitled to five rupees and eighty paise a day and issued instructions to the maliks to pay the same. Lachhman had landholdings at Tamadi, Burudiha, Kuruda, Hessadi, Chama and Dhai, and the villagers worked for him. Asrafi Mahato said, "We have not forgotten Karan and Bulaki. But the SDO seems to be good. Why should we fork for forty paise and a handful of grains? We don't want food. Let him pay us five rupees and fifty paise.

It alarmed Dulan. He tried to drive sense into Asrafi's head. "Karan had made a big noise and it led to the burning of the Dusad mohalla at Tamadi."

"Where is Karan, tell me, and where is Bulaki?"

"Who knows?"

"They are not alive."

"What makes you say this?"

"He killed them first and then threw them in some ravine in the forest."

"I don't know about that but see that the SDO is present when you negotiate with the malik."

"Well, I'll do that."

"See that the SDO does not leave station after the harvest. That time the malik paid the wages and took to arson later."

"I will ask him."

Lachhman was adamant. He said, "Two rupees plus tiffin."

"Malik Parwar, let us have only the wages."

"Ah, the wages!" Lachhman's eyes overflowed with sympathy and understanding. "Let me think a little, you people take some time too. Ah, even an ass knows that one should pay the revised wage-rate. Mentioned the SDO didn't you? Well, tell him that none of the local maliks are paying the new rate. If I do, it will ruin me."

Asrafi said in a humble voice, "Ruin you, malik? Who can ruin you? You have your own *attachaki*, wheat-grinder, one can see from a distance how tall your residence is."

To Lachhman his words were open defiance of his authority. He said, "We have talked among ourselves and have decided upon two rupees per day. The sarkar treats us like dirt simply because we hold a little land. You people get all the assistance, we receive none. Look at Dulan Ganju. I give him land and the scoundrel does not cultivate it. Takes paddy-seed and eats it. Let him! We receive nothing, have to buy everything beginning from fertilisers down to pesticides. Tell the SDO what I have said."

Asrafi told Dulan, "A word of caution, uncle. The malik knows that you do not cultivate that patch of land."

Dulan felt trapped. Lachhman asked him not to plough the land and Dulan could not say why. His tongue was kept tied. He felt alarming concern for Asrafi and told him, "Don't trust the malik, my son! Your father did the barber's job when my sons were born and I've known you since childhood."

"Now uncle, I won't."

Asrafi shuttled between the SDO and Lachhman. The signs were alarming and spelt disaster. Dulan's nerves were wrecked and he growled at his sons, "A lowcaste remains the same lowcaste cretin. Sitting here and eating off the old father. Waiting for whatever he gets out of the land. Had you been born different, you would have migrated to the coalfields long ago. Why are you rotting here, tell me?"

Dhatua raised his innocent eyes and said in a soft voice, "But father! This time we are getting double the usual."

Dulan found himself unable to talk further. He took it out on the BDO and told him curtly, "This time, I want financial assistance for the rabi crop." The BDO smiled toothily and said, "Yes, why not?"

"Babu, how come the papaya palm is so tall? It's very unusual."

"The palm was planted on the grave they dug to bury the mad dogs killed during summer."

"It's good fertiliser?"

"The best ever."

It lessened the deadweight weighing on Dulan. Returning to the village he went to his land. Yes, those tall lantanas and aloes!

Karan and Bulaki! His eyes filled with tears. Karan! He could not
kill you, you have come alive, raised your head. But why useless
plants? You fought for our rights, did you not? Then why could
you not change to wheat, or *marwa*, or maize, or paddy? Or to
cheena grass? We could have eaten the gruel made from cheena
grass seeds and remember you with gratitude?

Burning with suppressed fury he went to Tamadi. Finding no
one attending to Lachhman's vegetable garden, he drove some
buffaloes in so that they could feed upon the vegetables and entered the house. He told Lachhman, "Malik Parwar! Do write to
the doctor at the hospital to admit me. The wrecking cough and
pain in the chest."

"Later, after the harvest."

"As you say, malik!"

After the harvest! Others were going to be killed surely. Now
Dulan could do nothing but wait.

Harvesting began. The terms were two rupees and fifty paise
plus tiffin. Lachhman on horseback supervised the harvesting.
The police remained there to see that a situation endangering
"law and order" was not provoked. The *khetmazdoors* received
their weekly wages. The SDO, greatly relieved, left with the police.

The storm broke on the eighth day when Lachhman brought
khetmazdoors from outside for harvesting. Asrafi and the others
felt threatened and fear made them desperate and use strong
words.

"This you cannot do."

"Who says so? I am doing it, am I not, you sons of bitches?"

"But."

"I have allowed you to harvest and given you the wage agreed
upon. The game is over. Go home, scram!"

The outsiders laid down their sickles when Asrafi and the other
villagers threatened them and waited to see what happened.
Shooting began. The outsiders ran away. More firing.

How many died? According to Dulan and others, eleven, and to
Lachhman and the police, seven. Asrafi's father lost both the sons,
Asrafi and Mohur. Their names went into the file of missing per-

sons together with the names of Mohuban Koiri of Chama and Parash Dhobi of Burudiha. When the SDO entered the village, the relatives of the dead placed their heads upon his feet and cried. The SDO's face was hard and inscrutable. He himself showed the reporters around and assured the villagers that a police case would be filed against Lachhman. Lachhman was asked not to leave home till a warrant for arrest could be issued against him.

And in the moonlit night, when the wind was freezing cold and all was beautifully tranquil, Lachhman came to Dulan on horseback. It was a repetition of the past, all over again. Horses, nobles of animals, carrying four dead bodies. Lachhman's gunmen helping Dulan dig deep, deep graves. The rains of monsoon and the dew of autumn had made the soil soft and yielding to the strokes of the spade. Dulan buried Asrafi, Mohur, Mohuban and Parash, four missing persons, and felt them entering his consciousness. The weight was too heavy. Dulan was a frail man.

He became more weird. Now he demanded more seeds, more and more money for bullocks. And, after a month, giant-sized aloe plants and lantana bushes greeted him silently and offered him solace. They were the only evidence of a harijan *khetmazdoor* killing in a forgotten corner of south-west Bihar during the Emergency. Lachhman had to be released for want of evidence against him. Emergency! The SDO was demoted for provoking the *khetmazdoors* and for the deteriorating harmony between the malik and the mazdoors. Emergency! Lachhman and his caste-brethren offered puja at the temple of Hanuman Misra spending thousands on one hundred and eight *bel* leafs made of pure silver. Lachhman declared that if the sons and daughters of bitches wanted to work for him, they must not expect more than one rupee per head minus tiffin. Young men belonging to the youth section of the Congress became labour-contractors overnight. This time the *khetmazdoors* would have to pay twenty-five paise per head per day to the contractors from their wages. The young man promised to make the bastards work at gunpoint and burn anyone alive if he dared protest. Only such measures would bring peace in the area.

Dulan was all the while haunted by the memory of the dead. Should he migrate elsewhere with his sons? But where? Where, in south-west Bihar were the Dulan Ganjus safe from the Lachhmans?

On the Holi-festival day, he sat among the singing crowd like an outsider who had no belonging to the revelry. Slowly the revelry gave way to a hushed silence. Dhatua, saturated in *mowa*, the liquor made from the *mowa* flowers, was playing his string-instrument *tuila* and singing a song.

> Where is Karan?
> And Bulaki?
> Why can't anyone answer?
> For they have become missing persons on the police-register.
> Where is Asrafi Hajam?
> And his brother Mohur?
> Where are Mohuban and Parash?
> Why can't anyone answer?
> For they have become missing persons on the police-register.
> Karan had fought for a twenty-five paise rise.
> Asrafi's fight was for five rupees and forty paise.
> Bulaki and Mohur had just followed their brothers.
> Mohuban knew best to make *mowa*.
> Parash was the best dancer during the Holi.
> All, all have become missing persons on the police-register.

When Dhatua finished, there was a stunned silence. Dulan stood up, "Who has composed this song?"

"It's me, father."

Dulan burst into tears and said, "Forget this song, son. Forget it. Else you too will become a missing person on the police-register."

He walked to his land and stood amongst the wild plants. He whispered to the dead, "You have become a song composed by my son Dhatua, hear me? First weeds, then a song. Not paddy, nor cheena. Now do not haunt me anymore, I entreat you."

The aloes and the lantanas, bathed in the light of the full moon, seemed to be laughing. The refrain of Dhatua's song was carried to Dulan by the breeze. (But they were not missing persons on the

police-register. Dhatua knew the answer; but Lachhman had
made and kept him a captive.)

The Emergency was over. And paddy ripened into gold in
Lachhman's fields. This year there was a bumper harvest. The last
two years had witnessed drought and crop-failure. Raised plat-
forms could be seen everywhere in the fields. A good crop
tempted bird-life to the fields.

The mastans who were proud to be known as "congressi" till
now emerged this year as labour-contractors dropping the word
"congressi" from their names. A group of five, brandishing guns,
talked with Lachhman. Their leader was in terylene and had dark
glasses on. He spoke to Lachhman in the manner of Amitabh
Bachhan playing the role of a mercenary in some film.

"Your usefulness is over, see? Only the professionals will
handle the deals such as breaking a strike, supplying *khetmazdoors*,
supervising the harvest. I am the leader of the mercenaries in
south-west Bihar. Like it or not, you have to accept my offer. You
pay me five thousand, the entire sum in advance."

"Five thousand!"

"Then pay them the declared wages."

"No, I can't."

"You make a cool profit of eighty thousand rupees by not
paying them minimum wages. Why should you not pay me a
paltry five thousand?"

"I will."

"O.K. Now give me a list of the villages where your fields lie and
you get your mazdoors from. Any trouble maker?"

"No."

"Fine. I'll have to render my services to Makhan Singh and
Ramlagan Singh, too. And listen. You've to pay them one rupee
and twenty-five paise each, for my cut is twenty-five paise from
their wages."

"One rupee per head."

"One rupee and twenty-five paise as I said. My name is
Amarnath Misra and I don't waste time in idle talk."

"Are you related to Hanuman Misraji of Tahar?"

"His nephew. Uncle has provided with the initial capital for my venture."

Thus the terms were finalized. Hanuman Misra told Lachhman, "Yes, my nephew. When I purchased surface-collieries for my sons, I wanted to buy one for him too. He refused. Didn't want to encumber himself with rubbish, he said. An extraordinarily clever boy. His service is sought after by owners of factories... election-candidates... very competent. Has three wives in three towns and each of them has been provided with a house of her own. Was very close to the last ministry. It's a pity that none of my sons is like him."

Lachhman was a brute of a man, but he was not a fool. He realised that when a mercenary forced himself upon one, it was wise to accept him. What to do! Times have changed.

Harvesting began. No outsiders. Dhatua and the other villagers. One rupee and twenty-five paise wages and tiffin consisting of powdered *makai*, salt and chilli. Dhatua's mother gave her sons every day some pickle made from wild fruits. And Dulan sat and waited on his platform. The women sang as they harvested. The monotony of the song sounded like a soothing lullaby inducing one to sleep. But Dulan did not sleep.

What about sleep, Dulan?

Why does he not sleep?

Sleep for Dulan is found missing. Like those names on the police-register.

Trouble broke, expectedly, on the weekly payment day, when Amarnath Misra demanded his cut from the wages of the mazdoors. Lachhman said, "No violence, please. No cut-money from me either. Talk with them."

Amarnath bared his teeth like a hyena, "Talk? With them? You pay me." Dhatua took the lead and became the spokesman of the mazdoors. Lachhman was keen on avoiding a direct confrontation with Dhatua, Dulan's son. His method of dealing with an untouchable was to give him a bullet. This he could not do in Dhatua's case. Dulan was still useful to him.

Amarnath said, "I can't talk to these curs. Five hundred heads working for fifteen days. My cut comes to eighteen hundred and seventy-five rupees. Pay me."

"No malik, don't. We won't allow you to."

Lachhman sighed in exasperation. He would have to lift the gun again. Karan... Asrafi... and now Dhatua...

"Fifteen rupees for fifteen days, malik? Not eighteen rupees and seventy-five paise? Why, malik? Haven't we worked overtime to help you?"

Lachhman paid Amarnath and told Dhatua, "Don't raise your voice Dhatua, go home."

Karan was a fighter, Asrafi was courageous. Dhatua was very different. He never knew that he had the courage to fight with Lachhman over the issue of twenty-five paise cut for the mercenary till now. He told the villagers, "You people, go home. I'll talk to him and make him see sense."

To Lachhman he said, "From tomorrow no harvesting till we get our dues. We won't work and won't let you bring outsiders in."

"You should be thankful, Dhatua, that the police are here for their cut. Else... "

"What? You afraid of the police?"

Dhatua too left but his parting words made Lachhman furious. Yet he decided to give the untouchables another chance to make up their minds for Dhatua was the intermediary and he was Dulan's son. The villagers came the next day but they refused to work. Lachhman seethed with fury. The mercenaries had gone to Ramlagan Singh and Makhan Singh. It was not possible to get labour from outside at such short notice. Both the parties waited till sundown. Lachhman issued instructions to his gunmen. "Try to talk them into submission, don't take to shooting if you can avoid it." The gunmen of Lachhman, on horseback, entered the fields heavy and golden with paddy. The villagers waited for them.

"Listen, you sons and daughters of bitches... "

"You yourself are a son of a bitch... "

The gunmen raised their guns. The mazdoors ran into the fields and were swallowed by the paddy-plants. A quick exchange of words. Leading to firing. Frightened flocks of birds rising to the sky. A gurgle-like sound from the paddy-field. Someone found his throat choked with blood and was trying to spit it out. A missile of razorsharp sickles aimed at the legs of horses. The horses ran like mad. Latua and Param ran towards Tohri to report to the police.

Waiting for his sons was an insufferable agony to Dulan. Latua did not reach home till night fell.

"Where is Dhatua?"

"I haven't seen him. Why, isn't he back? I'd gone to the *thana*..."

"Dhatua, where is he?"

"We'd gone to fetch the police. Police will come to the village, know that? And that SDO remember him? He, too, will come."

"Dhatua!"

He could feel the dead ones moving, rolling over, making space for another. He stood up and broke into a run. His wife said, "Where are you going?"

"To my land."

"What! Dhatua is not back yet and you... his father... "

"Shut up your mouth, you bitch!"

Dulan ran. That song, composed by Dhatua... Where is Karan?... And Bulaki?... They have become missing persons on the police-register – Dhatua – his innocent eyes. Birthmark on the arm... do not become a missing person on the police-register, Dhatua, hear me? No, it can't be Dhatua... no...

Lachhman Singh. Kicking at someone with demoniacal fury. The man at his feet had blood all over his body. Two riders and three horses. Lachhman looked at Dulan.

"Dulan!"

"Dhatua?"

"What a pity, Dulan. I asked them not to, and this beast opened fire."

He kicked at the man again, "A trigger-happy mastan."

"Dhatua?"

"In the grave."

"Who buried him?"

"This beast."

"He?"

"Yes. But don't you dare open your mouth, Dulan. If you do, I will wipe out your family. And, and, come tomorrow... I'll pay you handsomely. Latua fetched the police. I'll purchase the police all right, don't worry, but I've let Latua go free because he is your son. I could easily have killed him, yet I didn't. Didn't touch the gun even once today."

They left. Lachhman and his gunman. Dulan sank down on the embankment, rolled down the slope, the swordlike leaves of the aloe plants tore at him.

This time there was no sudden hushing-up. Dhatua missing. Several wounded. The SDO intervened. The gunman and Amarnath both were sent to prison. Dhatua remained untraced.

And Dulan went mad. After the summer rains, he started pulling out the aloes and lantanas with savage fury. It alarmed his wife very much. Latua's wife told her that the old man had gone to the *zamin*, with a sickle and a shovel. Dhatua's mother forgot Dhatua and ran towards the *zamin*. She screamed at Dulan, "Have you gone mad? What are you clearing that land for?"

"Go back home."

"How can I?"

"Go back, I say."

Dulan's wife ran to the Pahan. The Pahan came with her and told Dulan, "Dhatua will come back, Dulan. Why are you acting crazy moping for him? Under the scorching sun too... "

"Go home, Pahan. Whose son is missing, yours or mine?"

"Yours."

"Who is the malik of this *zamin*?"

"You."

"I do not care whether you think me crazy or not. I am going to teach this *zamin* of mine a lesson."

"Ask Latua to help you."

"No, I have to do it myself."

The Pahan knew that he had lost the battle. He told Dulan's

wife, "Let him be. Let me take you home. You have to go to Tohri, remember?"

It was true. Dulan's wife went to Tohri *thana* from time to time to make enquiries about the missing Dhatua.

Dulan brought the paddy-seed home and declared that he was going to sow them. No eating this time. While scattering the seeds he went on whispering to the dead, "No more aloes and lantanas, Dhatua. Hear me? I am going to turn you all into paddy, hear me? Paddy... "

The villagers gathered on the embankment when the new shoots came up. They admitted that the plants on Dulan's fields were far superior to those on the malik's fields.

Someone said, "Had the malik been here, he would have been jealous."

"Who are you speaking of?"

"Lachhman Singh."

"Where is he?"

"With his in-law at Gaya."

"Is it so?"

Dulan had a bumper crop and, by early winter, the paddy ripened into gold. Then Dulan said, "I won't harvest."

His wife was furious, "What do you mean? Did you not labour like a demon all these months? And did I not carry meals to you every day?"

"No, I won't. And I strictly forbid anyone visiting me from now on."

"What will you do, just sit?"

"Yes, just sit... "

Squatting on the platform Dulan waited for Lachhman to return. He would have to, as his fields were ready for harvest. Lachhman learnt of Dulan's treachery on his return. He was furious. Dhatua had been dead for one year and Lachhman had got over it. He came to Dulan in the afternoon on horseback. Dulan knew that he would come. He was ready for the malik.

"Dulan!"

"Malik Parwar!"

"Come here!"

"How come you are all alone?"

"Don't be cheeky, Dulan. What is this?"

"What do you mean by 'what'?"

"Why have you sown paddy on the field?"

"Why should I not?"

"What were the terms of the agreement? Who gave you right to cultivate? Did I not ask you to leave the *zamin* as it is? Aloes and lantanas were all right... you son of a bitch..."

Dulan climbed up the embankment, Lachhman's legs dangling before him from horseback. He pulled at Lachhman's legs with all his might. Lachhman fell down crashing, his gun falling from his hands. Dulan took it up before Lachhman could stand up and brought down the butt of the gun on Lachhman's head. Lachhman screamed in pain. The butt crashed on his collarbone. Bones splitting under the impact.

"You son of a bitch... you beast... *janwar*..." Lachhman was shocked to discover that he was crying. Pain and fear. He, the almighty Lachhman, on the ground and Dulan, a Ganju, standing before him! He tried to grasp Dulan's ankle and sobbed with pain. Dulan had lifted a rock and crushed his fingers. Lachhman knew that it would take long to get the use of his right hand back.

"*Janwar*... beast... *kutta*... dog..."

"What were the terms malik, tell me? I am not to cultivate the *zamin*. Why? So that you can go on killing and I guard your secret. If I don't, you will burn the village and wipe out my family. Fine! Just fine! But malik, seven worthy human beings and only aloes and lantanas upon their graves? That is why I have sown paddy. They say I have gone mad. Yes, I have. Today I won't let you go, malik, I won't let you harvest, burn our huts and shoot people ever again. You have harvested enough."

"Will the police let you free?"

"Perhaps not, but who cares? Your men also might kill me. When did they not, tell me? Your mastans... police... let them. What can they do, kill me? But one has to die sometime... there is always a first time... did Dhatua die before he was killed?"

Lachhman knew that he was totally in Dulan's hands and he could smell death. It terrified him. But south-west Bihar is something very special. A Rajput here could not beg mercy from a Ganju even when death was imminent. Even if he did, a Ganju could not show mercy to a Rajput. Dulan could not.

Lachhman made a last effort to offer resistance. Dulan said, "What a pity, malik! Ultimately to be killed by a Ganju, a lowcaste!" He went on smashing Lachhman's head with a rock. Lachhman was a professional, knew the exact cost of a bullet. Killing did not disturb his inner-self. Dulan was not a professional. The rock cost nothing. He was killing Lachhman because only thus could he purify himself. He brought down the rock again and again till there was no longer any need to.

He stood up. There was a lot to do. He led the horse away and sent it flying by bringing down his stick upon the rump of the horse. Then he dragged both Lachhman and his gun to a distant ravine and threw both in. He covered Lachhman with rocks. Gusts of laughter choked him. To be buried, not burnt! A tribal funeral! What a pity! He hated the tribals and the harijans so!

He wiped off the dragmark and the blood with leafy branches of the lantana and went to sleep as soon as he lay on the platform.

Search for the missing Lachhman went on for a few days. Lachhman was not in the habit of taking anyone into his confidence, so none knew where he had gone. He never mentioned Dulan to anyone. His tenants could guess, of course, but better sense told them that it was futile to speculate as the malik himself, their protector, was missing. And anyway, the horse was found grazing on Dwaitari's fields. His servant said, "He had his glass of milk and left on horseback, that's all I know."

Surprisingly, the growls of hyenas fighting over the corpse attracted notice after a lapse of five days. When Lachhman was found at last, the hyenas had already made a meal of his face which they had managed to uncover. The cunning with which the corpse was hidden, plus the fact that the horse was found grazing on Dwaitari's field, led the scent to Dwaitari. Lachhman's son was convinced of Dwaitari's guilt. The past history of family-feuds supported his suspicion and Dwaitari was harassed for some days. Police gave up as there was little evidence against Dwaitari. The old family-feud was renewed with vigour. No one mentioned Dulan. Dulan was too ignoble, too small a person. How to associate him with the killing of a powerful malik? Dulan went to the Pahan to tell him something. He was grave, humble and calm. The Pahan noticed the change.

One afternoon the villagers were called to the Pahan's courtyard. Dulan addressed them. He had something to say. Shyly, haltingly, he said, "I have never gifted anything to anyone before... "

The villagers were not prepared for this. They were greatly surprised.

"You people admired the paddy I grew and called me crazy. But kindly listen to this crazy fool... "

"Speak... "

Lachhman's death had given them a sense of relief. It was too early to speculate what the malik's son would do. The villagers, for the time being at least, were at peace with the world.

"My harvest is seeds for you all. Do take it."

"You are giving away your paddy to be sown in our fields?"

"Yes. Do harvest the field. It's a long story... how I obtained such a magnificent crop."

"Used fertiliser?"

"Yes... very costly fertiliser, too. Do harvest my field... and listen, give me some too. I'll sow them, again and again... "

They assured him that they would do as he wished them to when the time came. Dulan felt greatly relieved and went to his field on quick, brisk steps. He stood upon the embankment to admire his field. The paddy was golden and magnificent being nourished by the flesh and bone of Karan, Bulaki, Asrafi, Mohur, Mohuban, Parash and Dhatua. Dulan climbed up the rickety ladder and sat upon the platform. The refrain of Dhatua's song haunted him.

"Dhatua... ," Dulan's voice shook. "Dhatua, hear me? I have changed you all into seeds... !"

YEARNING FOR THE FIORDS

by Teet Kallas

Teet Kallas was born in Tallinn in 1943. After serv-
ing in the Soviet army, he was a television and mag-
azine editor before becoming a professional writer.
He is the author of several novels, plays, children's
stories, newspaper articles, critical essays, and short
fiction pieces.

Translated by Aino Jõgi

T HE DAY is bound to come when once again you feel dog-
tired and disgusted as hell. Of course it takes time, but it will come
in due course. And then you lean your head – which seems to
have grown twice as large as it used to be, four times as heavy and
at least eight times as empty – you lean that poor head of yours on
your bony fingers, and gaze out of the window with a pained expression on your face.

Because there will be nothing to look at there. The back yard
with its view of a large block of apartment houses full of nooks and
curves. Garbage cans. Tracks leading up to them in the dirty end-
of-the-winter slush. Tracks running to the drum-shaped con-
tainers like bunches of straight spokes that look as if they were
drawn with a ruler, but a shaky one. Townspeople tend to leave
short scared stretches of straight paths in the snow.

But look at the footpaths in the countryside. Go across a field.

Follow a snowy track leading to some farm. Those tracks have been trodden by large warm felt boots of solid lined Wellingtons. Aren't they marvellous, those snowy tracks, with their fine curves and broad noble sweeps? Or else they zig-zag unaccountably. Where do they come from, all those sweeps and zig-zags? They are the work of the country people. A countryman walks, and as he goes, he breathes deeply. He walks and his eyes are open to everything around him.

Or take a forester. He may be wading through deep fresh snow, lost to his surroundings for quite some time, but all of a sudden he will stop. But why? To peer at an aspen over there on the hillside. Why? Because it's so beautiful that's why. Or perhaps he has startled a hare squatting under that aspen, a white hare that casts a long shadow on the sparkling snow as it scampers along. You cannot but halt in your tracks when a white hare leaps up unexpectedly, because it always looks deceptively large at first sight, as though it were not a hare, but some other animal.

And the forester goes his way, his mind busy with fresh thoughts, aspen thoughts and hare thoughts, and he isn't even aware that quite by chance, he has inscribed a neat curve in the pure snow. In half an hour the milkmaid will be going home to have some breakfast; she wears high rubber boots which make a nice crunching sound, and she doesn't have the heart to mar the bright snow with a fresh set of tracks. So she follows all the curves drawn by the forester. She even repeats the loop he made when he stopped to take a leak by the willow bush. The milkmaid pushes some fluffy snow on top of the yellow circle with the toe of her rubber boot without a shadow of resentment.

The third and the fourth and the fifth person to follow the same track each help to accentuate those curves and sweeps and loops, and if a week passes without a snowfall, a lovely, utterly puzzling footpath will emerge in the snow.

Why not go to the country to explore the tracks in the snow, you ask? But you need high boots for that. And you, my fellow townsman of the era of central heating, trot, comical and bashful, across the back yard to your garbage can in the dusk, taking a shortcut through the dirty slush, your galoshes squishing and the snow splashing onto your socks, and then you get the flu into the bargain.

Talk of the convenience of the central heating... But you haven't even a place to burn the rough drafts of your letters. You may be one of those people who are fond of letterwriting and polish their letters until they fairly gleam. The result will be a pithy and forcible message, but the rough drafts are enough to make you blush. They abound in awkward wordings, humiliating evidence of your inability and incompetence. Wouldn't it be fun if, having finished your letter, you could rake together all your mucked-up notes and with a firm and practised shake of the hand, strike a match to light the logs in your fireplace precisely and exclusively with those rough drafts? And then sit back and watch the eager flames lick and consume all proof of your inefficiency and lack of refinement. Like a pink-tongued cat over a saucer of milk, or a toy alligator with its red, mirthful, yet greedy jaws wide open, demanding none other than rough drafts! "I demand more rough drafts!" it would insist.

No, I've had enough of this, you'll say to yourself. I can't bear looking down into the back yard another minute.

It is tiresome and tiring each time you have to tear your rough drafts into a thousand tiny pieces and carry them to the garbage can. And there is no escape, for in an hour or two, the sooty dusk of the sunless day in early spring will be gathering, and people in galoshes will steal into their back yards trying to hide behind their backs buckets with the innards of spiced Baltic sprats and rough drafts of their letters.

Now doesn't this telephone look precisely as if it were going to ring shrilly in thirteen seconds flat.

You only manage to count up to eleven, and off it goes, that buzzing beetle on your desk. But no, you've had enough, you would refuse to pick up the receiver even if it were to buzz louder, even if it were to split your ears, because you're dog-tired and disgusted as hell. All you're going to do now is to evaporate quietly. You cross your room on tiptoe, your ears clogged with the jangle of the telephone. You struggle into your coat, wrap your muffler round your neck, pull your hat down across your eyes, stride down the long corridor with a resolute face, and plunge into a comforting world of colourful adventures and pleasant idle talk. Now you feel tired as a centipede. I'm speaking of myself now. Why a centipede? You see, it has to work harder to move; the poor thing has to wear out a whole set of legs; all hundred of them. Man, for instance, has only two legs to tire out. That means his life is fifty times easier than that of a centipede.

Where on earth did you pick me up, Madis? And who named you Madis, a fair, soft-sounding name to be sure? Oh yes, I remember. It was in that packed cellar where we indulged in a sweet discussion at an oaken table. It was men's talk. There are myriad things in this world to be discussed in such a leisurely way at an oaken table, over mulled wine and slated almonds. Look here, Madis, you're young and this is why you don't have as many things to discuss right now as I do. That's why you paused to listen to me talk, and that's why I'm here after all. That brown-eyed man served in my company. He lost an eye, but that doesn't mean he's any worse than the rest of us. It was a German bullet that knocked it right out of his head. Used to be a beautiful brown eye, but it stayed there in the mud of the River Emajõgi. I happened to be standing next to him. At the moment, we were discussing a third man's family troubles. He married that kind of woman. Yes, he was also from our company. Young and green when he joined up and just as young and green when he got back. Went like hotcakes. Young and too soft-spoken. The whole company was at the wedding party, what was left of it. Their one-room flat was large enough for us. Now that third man owns a large house, but happiness has left him.

With your permission, Madis, is this young lady your sister? Hm. I thought as much. I thought as much.

Let me sit here, basking in the glow of your fireplace, although in fact it is a stove, if I'm not mistaken. But let me think of it as a fireplace. And let me bask here, and you, sweet child, don't turn on that electric light hanging from the ceiling. And don't touch the TV-set, be a dear. I'm not in the mood for any TV-programmes tonight. I'd rather watch your sister. I hope she is your sister?

I see. She is. And her name is Sirje, fancy that.

I say Madis, you just go right on sipping the wine by yourself, and I'll take a minute to chat with your sister. You just go on with your newborn banquet, with your jubilation and celebration. As for me, I'd like to feel the warmth of the fire, sit back and squint my crow-footed eyes, and I'd like to commune with your sister.

I'd be more than happy to live in this wooden room – I made up the term right now from the term "wooden house." I'd just sit by the fire, quietly, without getting in anyone's way. But, of course – and now listen, I'm going to describe your profile. Remember the description so you'll know what you look like.

You're the Sirje of this dimly lit room. Point one. Since I know your elder brother, as we've managed to determine today, and with due respect for him and you and myself, and mankind, I'm telling you under his watchful eye and almost within his hearing, I'm telling you only calm, simple stories, calm and chaste as the sea in early October. You're seventeen, you ought to know what the sea is like in early October.

Well... There's something in your profile that confirms my hopes that you'll hear out my life's plans.

You've got the sweet snub nose of a Virumaa girl and grave eyes. When you smile, which for some reason you're doing just now, there's something in the way you curve your lips that goes straight to my heart. That smile shows you're no fool, but you're not affected either – which is very good. Yes. Good.

My life's plans are as follows: after I'm done with my suggestive preamble, your elder brother will pick up the phone, dial the necessary number and order a taxi. Then I'll leave with you. Your brother and the other young people, none of whom has so serious and carefully analysed a plan as I have by far, will come out onto the porch in their shirtsleeves. And as the taxi takes off, we'll wave to them amiably, perhaps even a bit regretfully.

And, you know what? At first I won't be sitting next to you in the back seat, but beside the driver since I'll have to explain to him where he has to take us and maybe even persuade him because it's a long way. From time to time, I'll cast appraising, encouraging glances your way as you huddle in the corner, perhaps a bit scared, too. And I would be immensely pleased if during the moments I manage to look at you, you turn your head so I can see your profile just like you're doing now.

I must confess, this scheme of mine, this plan has been incomplete thus far without your profile. But since your profile is in its proper place now, fitting in perfectly, outlined against the window on a spring night in this quaint wooden room, the gaps in my plan have been filled with miraculous ease; I'd even say with a certain elegance.

So there remains only one thing to worry me – who is to manage the punchcard factory for me? But never mind, we'll cross that bridge when we come to it. I'll just leave your brother Madis a note asking him to take over tomorrow. They're sensible people, most of them, and I believe they'll get used to Madis soon. True, the work is sometimes nerve-racking and, I can't conceal it, responsible. Still I trust Madis to make a success of it and assert himself – look at the promising shape of his nose and listen, just listen: his voice has the necessary dose of the metallic ring which is indispensable when one is to assert oneself, particularly when speaking over the telephone. While we're waiting for the taxi I'll try to explain to Madis what he'll have to face there – that is, of course, in case he gives his consent. It would take an immense burden off my shoulders if he were to agree. Oh, Sirje, perhaps you'll put in a word for me with your brother? How do you two get on, by the way?

Still, I'm full of optimism; I believe firmly in my enterprise. What about you, Sirje? And, Madis, would you be so kind as to order a taxi for me and Sirje, because, come to think of it, the hour's late, and taxis aren't easy to get. After all, we live in a large, busy town where everybody is in a hurry, don't we, my young friends?

It won't take me long now, Sirje; I'm getting nearer and nearer to my chaste and simple plan and, quite honestly, the thought of abandoning my family for the sake of it doesn't grieve me much, because, you see, once I tried to explain my plan to my wife, but she wouldn't so much as allow me to admire her profile and refused to see my point. Her attitude was one of complete detachment.

I have no desire to conceal the fact that I'm no longer young – I'm just forty-six, which should be borne out by the crow's feet near my eyes. But they won't disturb you I trust.

We're getting nearer and nearer.

Now, be a dear and shift this way a bit, keeping your head at about this angle – and try to keep a straight face because your smile won't let me concentrate, although I'm sure you don't mean any harm, for now that the taxi's on its way, I must tell you everything, briefly, precisely, keeping to the facts. By the way, perhaps some of the young people would be so nice as to pack your suitcases for you? And if you've got a pair of high warm winter boots, you should put them on soon. There now, that's a wonderful pose in the red glow of the fire. I've told you about the taxi; I'm going to skip the other vehicles we may need in the whirl of events, in the course of our adventures, but –

– and then, having done with my morning correspondence which, to tell the truth, is a slow job, but I'm set on improving myself – when I've written some letters to my dearest friends, brothers, nephews, acquaintances and my former office mates at the factory where your brother Madis, now also a close friend, will be in charge. We've known each other for several hours now and I'm sincerely delighted to have made his acquaintance – where was I? Oh yes, my correspondence. What shall I be writing about? My letter will certainly contain detailed descriptions of the interesting weather phenomena. So, when the hours allotted to my correspondence have passed, I will put the modest envelopes with the unassuming blue stamps on them into my drawer where there may be a hundred letters waiting to be mailed. Then, a little tired, but with a clear conscience, I'll go out.

It has taken us several months to build our yellow-walled log cabin. It has a red roof. I'm sitting on the porch, cupping my chin

in my hands and getting ready to meditate – just like this. Don't I
look great?

Over our cabin and me – I'm deep in thought at the moment –
rises the sky. Very high, very remote, very chaste and calm, a very
grave and awe-inspiring blackish blue sky. And I'm sitting here
and I feel – what do I feel? I feel a yearning for you. I'm overwhelmed by the noble feeling of solitude. And I sense the in-
finitely majestic sweep of the northern landscape. Then I leave for
a moment to fetch my violin from the room at the back of the
cabin. I return with the instrument pressed to my bearded cheek.
Seated on the porch, I tune my violin, growing very pensive, and
then begin to play. What should I play, in your opinion, when I'm
missing you? Sibelius. I have good taste, I've known since childhood that one can't get up and squeak out a gypsy romance under
this kind of sky.

I'm playing a sublime melody, and what do I feel? A longing for
you. The land is high, barren, stony. Just a few stunted trees –
some dwarf birches – clinging to the earth by their roots.

And below, there winds a footpath with perfectly unique curves
and sweeps, trodden by our own busy feet in the course of time.
And below it, I can hear the sea roaring. Which sea, you ask. The
sea of fiords. Sh-shah. Sh-shah. Sh-shah. Do you hear its peculiar
hiss and roar? And do you hear the sublime purity of the melody
I'm conjuring out of my violin? I'm not very good as yet, but I've
got the feeling that here under the fiord sky we might just merge
into one, my violin and I.

Then I shall listen for – but no, it was a fisherman's boat sailing
past about ten miles in the distance. There's only a small cutter
that calls on us once a month to pick up my letters and replenish
our food supplies. Sometimes we are sent books which we read in
the circle of light from our kerosene lamp, terribly slowly and terribly thoughtfully, turning them over in our minds and tasting
every word with intense enjoyment. . .

Right – at the moment I'm alone playing the violin.

And then – lo! it's you coming up the winding footpath from
the water's edge. I spot you at a great distance with my keen

sniper's eyesight. You're wearing a white top and a long, coarse, red woollen skirt. It's about the same colour as our roof. You are carrying a light white wooden tub under your arm with our freshly washed, simple linen. No frills, no laces, no scents, our bed linen is flaxen, and we lead the simple, chaste, pensive, unhurried life of the fiords.

Cautiously I place the violin on the porch and descend to meet you. Your face is as grave as it is now, but it cannot deceive me, for I know I need only to call your name, softly and gently, for a pure fiord smile to appear on your face of about the kind you're smiling now. But you haven't been to the fiords yet; that's why your smile isn't quite mature.

And as I advance toward you I think: good grief man – meaning myself – why haven't you done all that before? And look, isn't it pretty, the way she's climbing uphill from the fiord – I mean you. Is there anything more essential in the world than a solemn-looking, gentle woman ascending from the waterside carrying clean linen in a clean wooden tub under a clean arm, and over our heads, the darkling blue dome of the sky, so high and so low at once — seemingly so near you can reach out and touch it if you had the heart to spoil it, but you care too much... And all around you stretches the windswept stony terrain which I till stubbornly, with a kind of fiordy tenacity. Yes, and the woman is coming and I can openly go to meet her. So peaceful, so unhurried, so carefree... With the boundless sky over your head, as boundless as peace of mind.

And together we go to the kitchen table to dine on gruel of goat's milk and meal.

And now that I've told you my plan from beginning to end with utter frankness, you can pull on those high boots of yours, because right now the fiords are hemmed in with brilliant, fluffy snow. You can take along a couple of suitcases with your belongings and – there you are... the telephone's ringing, it must be our taxi.

Your elder brother Madis and all the other young folks are coming out to the porch to wave to us. We'll write to them. We can promise that, can't we?

Now I'll sit next to the driver, and you sit in the back as we decided. Yes, to the fiords please. Right, we've got to stop at my
place, I've got to take along one or two things. But, Sirje, where are
your suitcases? Never mind, we can borrow something from my
wife. Goodbye, my young friends. Madis, you go there at about
nine, a proper hour, and everything will fall in place. Goodbye, I
wish every happiness to you who are staying home. May good luck
and success attend you. But Sirje, where are you going... ?

The next morning found Viljam, the manager of the punchcard factory, aged forty-six, sitting at the kitchen table, lost in
thought. His wife was sending children to school; he could hear
their voices in the anteroom. Then she came into the kitchen,
poured another glass of kefir for Viljam, who was sitting with
clasped hands, and lightly tweaked a tuft of his short hair, perhaps
a bit too youthfully styled.

"So you've taken another trip to your fiords? You know the
penalty, don't you?" she said. "Before you go to work, you've got
to take out the garbage. The pail is full to the brim."

Viljam finished his glass of kefir, wiped his mouth, looked out
the window, and shook his head. There was a ghost of a smile on
his lips.

Crossing the yard on his way to work, he felt that the tiredness
and utter disgust had been swept away again for the time being.

FROM BEHIND THE VEIL

by Dhu'l Nun Ayyoub

Dhu'l Nun Ayyoub, born in 1908, is one of the leading writers of the early generation of realistic short
story writing in Iraq. He lives in Vienna.

Translated by S. Al-Bazzazz

THE STREET, although wide, was inconveniently full of
strollers passing to and fro. The situation was not helped by the
sleek swift cars, which sped by from time to time. They carried
wealthy occupants, young women and ladies, who, protected from
the curiosity of the outside world, displayed radiant faces. Their
shining gaze roved across the street, smiling or frowning as they
took in sights which pleased or displeased them.

Among the surging crowd was an amazing mixture of different
clothes and contrasting shapes, which, if nothing else, serve to em-
phasize the varying tastes of these passers-by.

A European who had never been to the East before might be ex-
cused for thinking that its people were in the middle of a great festival. As time goes by, however, he is moved to say in amazement,
"What long carnival celebrations you have in this country!" Our
Western friend would think that people wear these amazing

clothes for a festival, just as they would do in his own country.

You can also see women in the crowd, both veiled and unveiled. A man can be surprised to find himself turning involuntarily towards those figures, wearing long silk gowns, which give them such an enticing and alluring shape, and make the observer yearn to uncover the magic and the secrets which lie beneath them.

His desire is only increased when his gaze falls on the filmy veil. Behind it he can catch a fleeting glimpse of fine features and pencilled eyebrows, which serve to inflame the fires of his heart. It makes him want to devote the rest of his life to the exploration of this world full of shame-faced beauty.

Ihsan was one of those who would stroll along with the crowd displaying his smart and tasteful suit over his slim figure, patting his dark gleaming hair whenever he felt that the evening breezes had ruffled it, or spread a curl over his clear forehead.

This Ihsan was a young man of eighteen, good-looking with fine features which made him attractive to a number of women. Naturally he was aware of his appeal and attraction, and he had the youthful capacity to exploit it. That's why you can see him now, with his eyes wandering in search of a quarry.

Ihsan was not interested in chasing unveiled girls. They exuded poise, which he found unattractive, and they were always looking anxiously to avoid criticism so they never looked the passers-by directly in the face. They would walk by without turning their heads, paying no attention to the expressions of flattery which came their way from the gallants, who, after getting as much out of them as a dog gets out of barking at clouds, would give them no further attention.

This is the reason that makes Ihsan always sidle up to the girls with the long cloaks and the secret little movements which attract him: the burning sighs and the gentle laughter and the concealed glances.

Siham had gone out on the evening of that day as usual to take the air and stroll through the streets. This evening stroll had become a part of her life to such an extent that it was now indispensable. She couldn't remember exactly the date when she first set out to saunter through the street, and did not really know the reason why she kept up her evening appointments. If she did, she did not admit it. Whatever the case, no sooner had Siham seen the bustle in the middle of the street than she headed for the pavement. She looked cautiously left and right until she saw Ihsan in the distance, and suddenly she felt the blood coursing through her veins.

She found herself unconsciously moving towards him until she was almost parallel with him, saw him staring at her from top to bottom, and felt a tremor throughout her body. When she saw his burning stare almost penetrating the cloak which covered her slender body her heart beat violently. She was used to seeing him every day at this time, and she used to stare at him freely each time until she had memorized his face. Of late, she had begun to feel her heart pounding whenever she saw him, and her face flushed with confusion. There was nothing to stop her from feasting her eyes on him, however, because she knew that the veil covered her face and concealed the overwhelming attraction she felt for him.

We cannot be certain what it was that made this youth know that the girl was interested in him, and whether his first overture to her came in the course of one of his habitual overtures, which he made to any girl. Whatever it was, he went up to the girl boldly on that first day, and sidled up to her, greeted her, and saw her turning round to look at him cautiously before hurrying on her way.

He knew immediately that she was not angry with him, and emboldened, he carried on behind her and saw her going into one of the public parks. She knew that he was following her, and hastened on her way, trembling with conflicting emotions of joy, fear, and caution.

He followed her into the park for a short distance, until he saw her sitting on her own, behind a big tree. He went up to her and spoke to her smilingly.

"Good evening."

"Good evening," she replied shyly.

Then she raised her veil from her brown face and her dark eyes, and Ihsan was captivated by the long dark eyelashes which cast a shadow over her features.

The features of her face were fine, and inspired the beholder with the strongest feelings of awe and worship. She was fearful and breathless, turning from side to side like a timid gazelle. She knew that what she was doing amounted to an unpardonable crime, but drew comfort from one thing – the knowledge that this boy had not seen her before and did not know her. She was having an adventure, nothing more, and she was drawn into it by her youth and by the warm blood which coursed in her veins.

The boy's mind worked on some expressions of flattery and endearment. For his opening shot, he ventured: "I've seen you often, as you've passed by this street and then gone to walk among the trees. I wasn't able to talk to you because I respect you, and your whole appearance tells me that you are from a good family."

She replied, a little resentfully: "But I suppose you always try to talk with ordinary girls as well? Why don't you just chase the common girls, and satisfy your passions on them?"

"I'm sorry, really, I don't mean you any harm. But I'm alone, as you see, and I can't find a companion to share my walks with me. I saw that you were the only girl who found pleasure in these strolls, and so I felt that there was a link between us. Anyway, if you find my presence unpleasant in any way, I'll move off right now."

He made a move to get up, but she checked him and asked: "Do you know who I am?"

"I haven't the least idea, but this doesn't stop me from believing that I share your spirit," he replied softly.

"If you want to accompany me on these innocent walks, I don't see any objection," she mused. "There's no harm in strolling around with you for an hour or so, at intervals which we can agree on, on condition that you promise me that you won't try to follow me and try to find out who I am. I don't want to you trying to contact me at any other times."

"I respect your wish and I shall honour it," he replied formally.

The two of them sat side by side on one of the stone benches, and a deep silence reigned over them, in which each felt the beating of their own hearts. This silence continued for a long time.

Both of them had been overcome by the novelty of their strange and singular situation.

Ihsan, however, was a youth accustomed to flirtations, although he realized that this time he was faced with a girl who was pure and virtuous. There was something about her, a certain strength of purpose and character, which confused him, and stopped him from going too far. His mind worked to collect his thoughts and to rescue him from the situation into which he had unwittingly walked.

At length, he spoke, somewhat confused.

"What is your name, please?"

"Have you forgotten my condition that you should not try to identify me?"

"Of course. I'm sorry. But surely... in view of our future friendship... ?"

"Have you forgotten? We live in a society in which this situation is unforgivable. If my people knew anything of this they'd kill me. While society is like this, we must learn to deceive. We must use the follies of our society in order to break its shackles!"

"What a penetrating mind you have!" said Ihsan admiringly.

"Thank you. Time's getting on and I must be getting back to the house. I will see you again in two days."

As she said goodbye he tried to put his arm around her waist, but she rebuffed him sharply. Then she relented slightly, saying: "I don't know who you are. You might be one of those mean boys who take delight in trapping girls for their own pleasure and sport."

She went back to the house invigorated, but somewhat disturbed, for she had broken with the most binding and serious of traditions in one fell swoop. She didn't understand how it had begun and how it had ended, until it seemed to her that everything that had happened that day was a disturbing dream.

She threw her cloak on one side, and went to help her mother with the housework. She flattered her mother, made herself agreeable, and took delight in carrying out her orders and her ar-

rangements. When her father returned home from work she wel-
comed him with smiling face, then she went to her room to get on
with her studies.

She set about her work mechanically, with nervous high spirits,
and had disturbing dreams at night.

The meetings went on longer, and the subjects of their con-
versations diversified. The relationship between them developed,
and things became deeply involved. She no longer felt that there
was anything strange or unusual about the meetings, but she kept
her head, using her lively mind to conceal her relationship with
this boy, and to prevent him from trying to find out who she was
and getting in touch with her.

ONE DAY Siham was sitting with her father, talking to him after
supper, while he was scanning the evening paper. His eye fell on a
long article about women who had abandoned the veil, and, decid-
ing to have his daughter's view, he read the article out loud. No
sooner had he finished than Siham roundly abused the author for
trying to break with convention and introduce modern heresies.
Her father felt a greatly increased regard for his intelligent, well-
brought-up daughter, who obviously knew the value of traditions
and respected them. Such a difference between her and the rest of
her irresponsible, scandalous friends, who, no sooner had they
learned to read and write, went around throwing overboard society's conventions without shame or respect!

Impulsively, he moved towards his daughter and kissed her
forehead.

"God preserve you as a treasure for your father."

When she reached her room Siham could barely stop herself
from laughing out loud. She picked up her veil and danced with
glee, then stopped in the middle of the room and began to whisper
to the veil: "You black shroud, you know how I despise you and
make use of you to keep him apart from me! I don't care about
you, and I feel nothing for you. I defy you. But I love you too.
These poor girls take refuge behind you in order to preserve their

virginity, and their honour, and good morals. If they were more truthful they would say that they love you because you hide faults and scandals. I love you because you help me to enjoy my life in a way that only those who wear the veil can appreciate. I pity those wretched unveiled women. I scorn them."

T H E   S L A V E   F O R T

by Ghassan Kanafani

Ghassan Kanafani was born in 1936 in Acre. He is a
Palestinian writer and most of his work deals in one
form or another with the tragedy of Palestine. He
was killed in 1972 in Beirut by a bomb in his car.

Translated by S. Al-Bazzazz

HAD HE not been so sadly shabby one would have said of him
that he was a poet. The site he had chosen for his humble hut of
wood and beaten-out jerry cans was truly magnificent; right by the
threshold the might of the sea flowed under the feet of the sharp
rocks with a deep-throated, unvarying sound. His face was gaunt,
his beard white though streaked with a few black hairs, his eyes
hollow under bushy brows; his cheek-bones protruded like two
rocks that had come to rest either side of the large projection that
was his nose.

Why had we gone to that place? I don't remember now. In our
small car we had followed a rough, miry and featureless road. We
had been going for more than three hours when Thabit pointed
through the window and gave a piercing shout:

"There's the Slave Fort."

This Slave Fort was a large rock the base of which had been

eaten away by the waves so that it resembled the wing of a giant bird, its head curled in the sand, its wing outstretched above the clamour of the sea.

"Why did they call it 'The Slave Fort'?"

"I don't know. Perhaps there was some historical incident which gave it the name. Do you see that hut?"

And once again Thabit pointed, this time towards the small hut lying in the shadow of the gigantic rock. He turned off the engine and we got out of the car.

"They say that a half-mad old man lives in it."

"What does he do with himself in this waste on his own?"

"What any half-mad old man would do."

From afar we saw the old man squatting on his heels at the entrance to his hut, his head clasped in his hands, staring out to sea.

"Don't you think there must be some special story about this old man? Why do you insist he's half-mad?"

"I don't know, that's what I heard."

Thabit, having arrived at the spot of his choice, levelled the sand, threw down the bottles of water, took out the food from the bag, and seated himself.

"They say he was the father of four boys who struck it lucky and are now among the richest people in the district."

"And then?"

"The sons quarrelled about who should provide a home for the father. Each wife wanted her own way in the matter and the whole thing ended with the old man making his escape and settling down here."

"It's a common enough story and shouldn't have turned the old man half-mad."

"There he is, only a few yards away – why not go over and ask him?"

Thabit looked at me uncomprehendingly, then lit the small heap of wood he had arranged and poured water into the metal water-jug and set it on the fire.

"The important thing in the story is to agree about whether his flight was a product of his mad half or his sane half."

Thabit blew at the fire, then began rubbing his eyes as he sat up straight resting his body on his knees.

"I can't bear the idea which the sight of him awakens in me."

"What idea?"

"That the man should spend seventy years of his life so austerely, that he should work, exert himself, existing day after day and hour after hour, that for seventy long years he should gain his daily bread from the sweat of his brow, that he should live through his day in the hope of a better tomorrow, that for seventy whole years he should go to sleep each night – and for what? So that he should, at the last, spend the rest of his life cast out like a dog, alone, sitting like this. Look at him – he's like some polar animal that has lost its fur. Can you believe that a man can live seventy years to attain to this? I can't stomach it."

Once again he stared at us; then, spreading out the palms of his hands, he continued his tirade:

"Just imagine! Seventy useless, meaningless years. Imagine walking for seventy years along the same road; the same directions, the same boundaries, the same horizons, the same everything. It's unbearable!"

"No doubt the old man would differ with you in your point of view. Maybe he believes that he has reached an end which is distinct from his life. Maybe he wanted just such an end. Why not ask him?"

We got up to go to him. When we came to where he was he raised his eyes, coldly returned our greeting and invited us to sit down. Through the half-open door we could see the inside of the hut; the threadbare mattress in one corner, while in the opposite one was a square rock on which lay a heap of unopened oyster shells. For a while silence reigned; it was then broken by the old man's feeble voice asking:

"Do you want oyster shells? I sell oyster shells."

As we had no reply to make to him, Thabit enquired:

"Do you find them yourself?"

"I wait for low tide so as to look for them far out. I gather them up and sell them to those who hope to find pearls in them."

We stared at each other. Presently Thabit put the question that had been exercising all our minds.

"Why don't you yourself try to find pearls inside these shells?"

"I?"

He uttered the word as though becoming aware for the first time that he actually existed, or as though the idea had never previously occurred to him. He then shook his head and kept his silence.

"How much do you sell a heap for?"

"Cheaply − for a loaf or two."

"They're small shells and certainly won't contain pearls."

The old man looked at us with lustreless eyes under bushy brows.

"What do you know about shells?" he demanded sharply. "Who's to tell whether or not you'll find a pearl?" And as though afraid that if he were to be carried away still further he might lose the deal, he relapsed into silence.

"And can you tell?"

"No, no one can tell," and he began toying with a shell which lay in front of him, pretending to be unaware of our presence.

"All right, we'll buy a heap."

The old man turned round and pointed to the heap arrayed on the square rock.

"Bring two loaves," he said, a concealed ring of joy in his voice, "and you can take that heap."

On returning to our place bearing the heap of shells, our argument broke out afresh.

"I consider those eyes can only be those of a madman. If not, why doesn't he open the shells himself in the hope of finding some pearls?"

"Perhaps he's fed up with trying and prefers to turn spectator and make money."

It took us half the day before we had opened all the shells. We piled the gelatinous insides of the empty shells around us, then burst into laughter at our madness.

In the afternoon Thabit suggested to me that I should take a cup of strong tea to the old man in the hope that it might bring a little joy to his heart.

As I was on my way over to him a slight feeling of fear stirred within me. However, he invited me to sit down and began sipping at his tea with relish.

"Did you find anything in the shells?"

"No, we found nothing – you fooled us."

He shook his head sadly and took another sip.

"To the extent of two loaves!" he said, as though talking to himself, and once again shook his head. Then, suddenly, he glanced at me and explained sharply:

"Were these shells your life – I mean, were each shell to represent a year of your life and you opened them one by one and found them empty, would you have been as sad as you are about losing a couple of loaves?"

He began to shake all over and at that moment I was convinced that I was in the presence of someone who certainly was mad. His eyes, under their bushy brows, gave out a sharp and unnatural brightness, while the dust from his ragged clothes played in the afternoon sun. I could find not a word to say. When I attempted to rise to my feet he took hold of my wrist and his frail hand was strong and convulsive. Then I heard him say:

"Don't be afraid – I am not mad, as you believe. Sit down. I want to tell you something; the happiest moments of my day are when I can watch disappointment of this kind."

I reseated myself, feeling somewhat calmer.

In the meantime, he began to gaze out at the horizon, seemingly unaware of my presence, as though he had not, a moment ago, invited me to sit down. Then he turned to me.

"I knew you wouldn't find anything. These oysters are still young and therefore can't contain the seed of a pearl. I wanted to know, though."

Again he was silent and stared out to sea. Then, as though speaking to himself, he said:

"The ebb tide will start early tonight and I must be off to gather shells. Tomorrow other men will be coming."

Overcome by bewilderment, I rose to my feet. The Slave Fort stood out darkly against the light of the setting sun. My friends were drinking tea around the heaps of empty shells as the old man began running after the receding water, bending down from time to time to pick up the shells left behind.

THE DRUMMING SANDS

by Ibrahim Al-Kouni

Ibrahim Al-Kouni was born in 1948 in Ghadames, Libya, and graduated from the Gorki Institute in Moscow. He has published essays, criticism, and short stories.

Translated by Denys Johnson-Davies

MISBAH SAID jumped down from the Land-Rover and took out a blanket and spread it under a sparse desert tree. He watched his companion opening the front of the Land-Rover, examining the oil and letting the motor cool off. He gave an encompassing look at the emptiness, silent and surrendered to the sun, while the sound of the engine still buzzed in his ears. "Jabbour," he said, collapsing onto the blanket, "you wouldn't have an Aspro, would you? The noise of your car has given me a headache." He spat onto the sands that glistened under the sun's rays and watched the spittle disappear into the thirsty pores.

"I feel my brain's boiling," he added.

Jabbour approached with a loaf of bread, tins of sardines and a bottle filled with a yellow-coloured liquid.

"You people of the city aren't used to the desert. Wait, I've got nature's cure for headaches and all other illnesses, a medicine a lot more effective than Aspro."

"Whiskey in this heat! God forbid!"

"We'll rest here until the evening," said Jabbour, engrossed in opening the tins of sardines, "then we'll continue our journey by night. It's better both for us and the car."

He broke the loaf with his hands, then opened the bottle and poured out two glasses.

"Let's agree as from now," he said, handing him the glass – "you have two to my one. Don't forget I'm driving – also I'm not a drinker like you."

"And who told you I was a drinker?"

"You're a man of the city, besides I don't believe your life in Europe was devoid of such things. As for me, I'm still a student, and were my father to find out he'd immediately take his gun to me – this despite the fact that he used to imbibe *laqbi* in his time. Ah, how cruel were our fathers, killing a date palm in order to get drunk from its heart."

"Ah, Europe... " said Misbah Said, as though talking to himself.

Jabbour took a sandwich and Misbah Said added in the same tone:

"Europe, it took me over. I was like you."

"Leave talk of Europe till after the third glass," Jabbour interrupted, handing him his second glass. "It's a subject that greatly interests me. They promised to send me on a scholarship to France so as to further my career as an agricultural adviser. An agricultural adviser – what a job! Do you know how tedious it is? Ough, those Touareg refuse to participate in any agricultural project. They still believe themselves to be aristocrats, knights of the desert, and despise farming and farmers."

He took a bite at the sandwich and mouthed the words as he chewed:

"But... they're good people... one must... help them."

He turned towards Misbah Said, who was leaning against the

trunk of the tree and looking at the far horizon, a shimmering mirage.

"You seem to be worried. Don't think of Europe now. I told you, after the third glass. The third glass will make you reveal to me those secrets you don't want to reveal."

"In Europe there aren't any secrets."

"We shall see. We shall see. You seem to be worried despite the second glass. Ah, I've remembered – what's your opinion of the Governor of Ghat? It'll be a journalist's scoop. He's a modest man and didn't tell you how alone, with his three children, he was able to hold up a French unit of armoured cars in the aggression of 'fifty-seven. A fabulous man – don't forget this incident in your investigation."

"I was like you," Misbah interrupted him in a dreamy voice, "before I went to Europe."

He took the glass from Jabbour.

"Don't go to Europe," he asserted firmly. "I don't advise you..."

Jabbour raised his head enquiringly. Taking a cigarette from Jabbour, he added:

"It's difficult to explain."

"Even after the third glass?"

"After even the tenth."

For several minutes there was silence. Wiping the sweat that poured from his brow with the sleeve of his shirt, Jabbour said:

"I hope that you will take back with you some good copy about life in the south. I must say you're the first journalist to take his profession seriously in this country."

Misbah Said watched the smoke from his cigarette floating in the air.

"Yeah," he answered in a despairing tone, "but I don't see any point in it all."

Jabbour came and sat down beside him.

"Perhaps," he said confidentially, embracing the vast emptiness with his gaze. "But I don't see it like that. We are always capable of doing something for those unfortunate people. They are content with their misery, submitting to their misfortune as though it were God's destiny for them. Our task is to demolish in them this contentment, to make them believe that that evil lieutenant and his ally the Governor are no more than a couple of dummies who are appropriately employed sitting on chairs and writing suspect reports to the powers-that-be. It's difficult to demolish this contentment, but it's our duty to try."

He drew on his cigarette and added:

"The press is one of the tools by which to bring it about."

"The lieutenant's a good man."

"Good?"

After a period of silence he added: "Good people don't kill."

"Kill?"

"Certainly. He killed and wounded sixty-four people in the demonstrations. Till now he hasn't forgiven me for having arranged those demonstrations. He tries to show affection for me but it's all a show – mere show and malice. He doesn't forget that they stripped him of two pips because of this crime, and he believes that I am still actively political among the people. As you see, one's personal interests are stronger than anything else."

Astonishment showed in Misbah's eyes but he kept silent. He was looking at the mirage wrestling with the silence, the sands and the labyrinthine horizon. The sun was beginning to set as the Land-Rover set off across the emptiness that stretched away endlessly.

"The desert – how dreary and frightening it is!" said Misbah as he looked out at it through the window.

Holding hard to the steering wheel, Jabbour commented:

"Yes, it's dreary and frightening, but it's like life, like existence itself, a secret that seems to be sunk in desolation and silence. It promises you everything, it promises you the most priceless thing that can be given to a traveller who has lost his way. It promises you water and when you look for the water all you find in front of you is a mirage – mirages and mirages, a sea of mirages. They dance in front of you and stick their tongue out at you in mockery, leading you on without purpose. But, mind, you must always resist. Don't give in to the mirage as being a mirage, for the desert mirage is nothing but an underlying enigma, behind which you must search for real water. Don't let despair take possession of you, for in the end, over there, behind that endless mirage, you will find a well, if not a complete oasis. The great thing is to resist – that's the first secret for dealing with the desert."

He turned toward Misbah and asked him to light him a cigarette. After a period of silence broken only by the buzzing of the engine, he said:

"The desert's like a flirtatious woman. It is unassailable, coquettish, never giving itself from the first time. You must try to possess it, try to discover its secret so that you can make yourself master of it. You see no point in all that. I, though, I see the point in everything. It is this that the desert has taught me. As for Europe, it has taken you over because you submitted to it."

Misbah made no comment whatsoever. He continued to watch the darkness flooding the emptiness, listening to the hum of the motor that bored into his ears and brought on his headache.

Jabbour stopped the car alongside a small sandy hillock. He got down, climbed the hillock and looked about him.

"It's the middle of the night," he said, coming back down, "and I don't see any sign of the lights of Oubari. It seems we've lost our way."

Jumping down from the car, Misbah said in a tone of annoyance:

"We should have kept to the main road from the beginning."

"Say rather that we shouldn't have got drunk – that's more to the point." Jabbour laughed and threw himself down on the soft sands and took out the packet of cigarettes from his pocket.

"I wanted to take a short cut," he said quietly, having lit the cigarette. "I relied on my experience but it appears that the desert doesn't excuse those who are drunk. If you want us not to commit a fourth mistake, then we must remain here till dawn. There's not enough petrol left to allow us to roam around the desert aimlessly. We haven't got sufficient reserves of petrol. That's our third mistake and the worst mistake of all. Come along, my dear fellow, tonight you're going to find yourself obliged to talk to me about Europe, if only to wile away the long night."

He laughed cheerfully but stopped as he noticed Misbah's annoyance. The latter had collapsed on the cold sands and was looking at the sand dunes submerged in dark silence.

"The moon will soon show her face," said Jabbour, as though to reassure him, having realized the reason for his unease. "You'll see how magical the desert looks at night by moonlight. You'll enjoy its magic as it bares itself to you like a European woman. It will reveal to you one of its many secrets, as numerous as the grains of sand."

MISBAH SAID listened intently. It seemed to him that the beating of drums and the noise of music pierced his ears, coming from somewhere close by, very close, from just behind or from on top of the sand hillock. Again he listened carefully: the beating of drums was more violent, the reverberation of the music more clamorous. It was an African rhythm, African drums – violent, clamorous, frenzied and mournful.

Misbah Said was so agitated that he was frightened he would divulge to his companion what he was hearing.

He made up his mind to occupy himself with something so as to drive away the hallucination and began to sing an old folk song.

THE MOON with its pallid mien began to steal out from behind the sand hillock. Still in the grip of his agitation, Misbah enquired:

"Jabbour, don't you think there are tribes living near here? The Touareg, for instance?"

"The Touareg don't live in the open air," Jabbour said as he stretched out lazily on the sand, smoking a cigarette. He crossed his legs and looked out into space. "These wastes are inhabited only by wolves and silence and various reptiles. That's at night – as for daytime there's the sun and the mirages."

"How strange! It seemed to me a short while ago... " He hesitated before making known his secret: "I heard the beating of drums and music being played on some weird instrument."

"You see," commented Jabbour with a smile, "this is the first of the secrets."

"You're joking."

"I'm not joking," Jabbour broke in seriously. "These are the drums of the desert."

"Drums of the desert?" asked Misbah in a childish tone. "You're making fun."

"I'm not making fun. The desert's a living being, like man. It has a soul and a spirit and pores to its skin. It suffers. It dances at night, it sings, it beats drums, plays music. It cheers itself up, generally after the torment of an intensely hot day. You don't know the desert, Misbah."

Misbah kept silent and Jabbour rose and turned towards the pallid moon.

"You don't know," he added, "the secret of the success of African music – it's because it's drawn forth from the bowels of this desert. They knew that looking at it would drive them to madness, so they participated with it in its dance and its joy and thus they conquered it by conquering their own fear of it. Had they maintained the attitude of the onlooker they would have been gripped by terror and madness. They deal with it as they deal with life. I confess that I was gripped by terror the first time I heard those drums, but after that I got used to them."

"I've never heard about it before."

"And you won't hear about it. You city-dwellers, you isolate yourselves in your cities and complain about life and other things, so how do you hope to understand the desert? I've told you, the desert's a woman whom it is difficult to know from the beginning. You need to be on intimate terms with her for a longer time if you are determined to discover her secret."

He pulled off his sandals and plunged his hands and feet into the cold sands.

"How sad this desert is!" he said in a choked voice. "It is tortured by day, its bones being crushed by the sun. It makes complaint of its eternal sadness by playing magical tunes on the tiny particles of sand. It plays and plays, beating the drums until morning overtakes it, when once again it throws its body into the arms of its executioner, the sun. And so the journey of eternal torment continues."

Jabbour had his head lowered towards the ground, his hands and feet thrust into the cold sand. It seemed to Misbah Said that he would burst into tears. He went on regarding him in silence, then there penetrated to his ears the sounds of drumming – surging, sad and frenzied.

B E F O R E reaching the main road they were out of petrol. Jabbour jumped from the Land-Rover and took down with him the gallon of water.

"Having been in touch with the police post at al-Uwainat they'll come to our rescue. We must reach the main road by foot before they start their search."

"Leaving the road was a mistake from the start."

"The real mistake was getting drunk. I'm feeling thirsty already. I committed a sin the desert won't forgive me."

He carried the water and they moved off in the direction of the main road.

I T W A S midday. The sun had drawn close to the desert's body, its flames unleashed. The last drop of water had gone but they hadn't yet reached the main road.

M I S B A H sat on the scorching sands to recover his breath, while Jabbour wiped the sweat away with his fingers and stared out at the vastness that stretched before him.

"I'm not going anywhere," said Misbah, trying to moisten the walls of his mouth and his dry lips with a parched tongue. "I can't make it."

Jabbour stretched out his arms to help him, but the latter firmly shook his head in a sign of refusal.

H E H E A R D him talking, then sitting down alongside him, then talking and talking and continuing to make gestures with his hands, but he no longer heard, was no longer listening, no longer seeing. Everything was immersed in darkness as Jabbour carried him on his shoulders. He would stagger and fall and then he'd drag him along by his feet, and the soft sands would frenziedly set up their sad, raucous music.

THE SUN's disk plunged down to embrace the horizon in an orange glow. The burning rays, ablaze like skewers, had beaten down the whole day on the township. With the lifting of the heat the reptiles and insects came out of their hiding-places to move around amongst the bushes, the areas of wasteland and the date palms. The people who had kept to their huts also came out and went to their cultivated fields and started up the pumps to fill the parched waterways.

In the courtyard in front of the guest-house a number of the inhabitants had gathered, with their large white turbans, to gaze curiously through the windows.

The Land-Rover arrived, raising behind it a long trail of dust. The inhabitants ran off to hide themselves among the date palms behind the municipality building. The lieutenant's tall form stepped out; he was dressed in uniform and two silver pips shone on his shoulders; in his right hand he carried a cane. He came to a stop in the courtyard of the guest-house and stood there for a while before entering.

"How do you feel now?" he asked without emotion, seating himself on a wooden chair.

Misbah Said sat up in the bed, leaning his back against the wall.

"Thanks be to God," he said, "I'm getting my strength back. What's the latest news?"

The lieutenant took out a packet of cigarettes and offered one to Misbah Said, who repeated his question as he lit a match for the lieutenant:

"What's the latest news?"

"Nothing new. I received the last call a short while ago – they haven't found anything yet. Cars are still out scouring the desert."

The silence was pierced by the clamour of the crickets and the murmuring of the inhabitants who were again swarming round the house.

"You should ally yourself with them."

"I'm afraid the time has passed," the lieutenant replied to the suggestion. Outside the clamour of the crickets and the noise of the pumps grew louder in the silence. Then the lieutenant repeated:

"I'm afraid the time has passed."

T H E   H U M of the pumps had grown silent, the inhabitants had taken themselves to their huts, and the night had become a stage for insects and reptiles and the silence broken by the persistent lament of the crickets. Seating himself cross-legged on the Persian carpet – he was dressed in civilian clothes – the lieutenant was preparing the green tea over a fire of hidden embers.

"They found him drowned in the well," he said. "He was totally naked."

He denuded the coals of ashes with a fan made from palm fronds, and went on in a low voice:

"You know that thirst makes a man imagine that his clothes are so heavy on his body that he wants to free himself of everything. He does so as the moment draws near when man gets rid of his complex of being embarrassed to walk about naked."

"Thirst," he went on after a few moments of silence, "thirst makes him forget that there's absolutely no point in arriving at the well without clothes. He would have been able to tear them up and make of them a rope which he could have let down into the well and sucked at the wet cloth. But he had freed himself of the clothes and thus faced a cruel choice: either to die of thirst above the well as he looked down at the water or to die of drowning in the water, that's to say in the well."

"He began stirring the tea. Without attempting to change his indifferent tone of voice, he continued:

"You can imagine what it means for a man to cover fifty kilometres only to die, far away over there, in the bottom of the well. He had resisted for a long time and had only thrown himself into it when he had lost all hope and was in a state of madness."

He passed Misbah the tea in a small glass, which Misbah placed on the rug in front of him. He remained silent, his back in contact with the cold wall as he listened to the lament of the crickets outside. With his thumb he traced along the pattern adorning the Persian rug, then said quietly:

"You know, lieutenant, I heard a story about something that happened in al-Hammada al-Hamra at the time of the drought and famine. A bedouin met up with a robber under the open sky. The brigand wanted to rob him of his only camel, so the bedouin pleaded with him saying that it was the only one he possessed and promised to take him to a rich man of his acquaintance who was in need of someone to herd his camels and sheep. On the way to the rich man's village the robber trod on a mine that had been left over from the World War. When the robber felt the mine under his feet the emotion of human kindness was awakened within him and he told the bedouin to make good his escape. But the bedouin, amazed by the robber's humanity, insisted on digging a deep hole under the robber's feet. Having finished it, he told his companion to fall backwards into the hole just as soon as he had gone off to a sufficient distance. The bedouin went off until he was out of sight of the robber. The robber then withdrew his foot and fell into the ditch behind him. However, a stray piece of shrapnel struck the bedouin a mortal blow, while the robber escaped without a scratch. Do you understand me, lieutenant?"

"I understand you. I understand you."

"It's always the innocent who die and the robbers who are left. Do you understand me, lieutenant?"

"I understand you. I understand you. Life... life – like the desert – knows no mercy. Life is a crime in the desert. I saw that written up in Tifinagb[1] on the walls of Mount Akakus and it was translated to me by a learned Sheikh from the Touareg."

1. The script of the Tareef.

Misbah Said remained with his back in contact with the wall. After a few moments drumbeats burst forth from the bowels of the silence, a rhythm that was violent, raucous and frenzied, yet at the same time deeply sad.

THE BEATS followed one another, and voices were raised in song: a strange singing that resembled wailing. He heard shouts and groans mixing with the singing and the clamour of the drums. He tried to drive the noise from his head. Despite himself he asked:

"Don't you hear the beating of drums?"

"Of course I hear it – it's the Touareg singing."

"The Touareg?"

"The Touareg get together every week, on Fridays after midnight, to sing and dance to their drums until the morning. These are their customs."

Then he rose and put on his shoes.

"You must rest. Tomorrow there's a long journey ahead of you."

He closed the door behind him. After a while Misbah heard the sound of the Land-Rover's engine mingling with the beating of the drums. He listened for a few moments, then dressed and went out.

HE THREADED his way through the date palms immersed in darkness. He cut across the cemetery. Behind a sandy hillock he saw women garbed in black sitting in a circle round the drums and veiled men with large white turbans who were dancing, calling out to one another, and going into convulsions and striking their breasts with their fists.

He squatted down on top of the hillock and watched their frenzy and listened to their raucous drumming, their pained groans, their songs that were as sad as laments for the dead. The din pierced the darkness, the desert and the quietness of night.

The winds woke him early as they buffeted the glass of the windows and the doors. He sat waiting in the reception hall, with the dust embedding itself in his hair and round his neck and creeping in between his body and his clothes.

The lieutenant came in. He was wearing his summer uniform. Without greeting him he asked:

"Are you ready? We must set off before the storm gets worse so as to catch the afternoon plane. I've decided to take you along myself."

The lieutenant sat behind the steering wheel and drove the Land-Rover at a dangerous speed for such a day when, with the dust, visibility was no more than three metres. A quarter of an hour passed without them exchanging a word, then the lieutenant asked:

"If you'd be kind enough, a cigarette."

Misbah Said took the packet of cigarettes from his pocket and lit one for the lieutenant and one for himself. Drawing on his cigarette, the lieutenant said:

"One must enjoy everything." Then he coughed and added: "Even smoking."

"Yes, one must enjoy everything," commented Misbah mockingly. He affected a cough and added in imitation of the lieutenant's tone of voice: "Even committing a crime."

The lieutenant's lower lip trembled as he turned sharply to his companion.

"What?" he asked in surprise. "What do you mean?"

"Nothing."

He pressed down again on the accelerator as a silence rose up between them.

MISBAH's face was flushed as he said with alarming calm:

"Why did you kill him?"

"I don't understand you."

"You do. The people told me everything yesterday."

After a moment of silence the lieutenant answered:

"The people! Perhaps they told you of some alleged enmity between him and me?"

"No, they told me of things other than the enmity."

"I don't understand you."

The silence had risen up between them like a mountain, but Misbah Said seized hold of the lieutenant's arm in a sudden convulsive movement as he shouted:

"You understand all right... you understand."

The lieutenant had to brake and bring the car to a complete stop. Without his features expressing any anger or agitation he removed the hand that clutched at his arm.

The dust storm had worsened so much that it was impossible to see ahead at all. The lieutenant preferred to wait till the storm calmed down and brought the car to a stop at the side of the road. He took out a packet of cigarettes and offered one to Misbah, who refused with a shudder. The lieutenant lit his own cigarette and said quietly through the cloud of smoke:

"There are many things you don't know about, very many things."

"But I know many things. It is enough for me as from today to know that a man of the law can commit a crime before the world and remain free."

"Do you consider that a crime?"

"Yes, it was possible for you to have saved him."

"A man of the law is not responsible for saving anyone."

"But you are responsible, in fact you're under an obligation to do so."

"Now we're getting close. Listen. Listen well. A man who chooses the life of the desert must not rely on anyone. Because he is not subservient to anyone's authority, he enjoys utter freedom, even if he doesn't know what to do with this freedom except to chase after gazelles or mirages. When he's thirsty or in difficulties he must rely on himself, he must pay the price of the complete freedom he enjoys because of his being free of authority."

Misbah Said began to tremble. He drew close to the lieutenant as he said:

"Had Jabbour been free of authority he would not have depended on you."

They exchanged a quick glance before the lieutenant said:

"Had he been subject to authority, why did he dare to raise his voice against me so as to win over those idiotic locals to his side? He knew that no one would come to his rescue for the Touareg had taught him to lead an ascetic life and choose the desert, and his death was the price for defending this freedom. This authority does not protect those who raise their voices in opposition to it. So long as the authority provides you with bread and takes upon itself to care for you and look after you and protect you, it will certainly break your head in if you try to show enmity. It makes payment to you in exchange for your keeping quiet, it buys your eternal silence, but if you've taken your freedom then all you can do is to have recourse to the desert."

"Your justification is barbarous, uglier than the crime," said Misbah in a threatening tone. "But wait – you'll see when I arrive at the capital. I'll expose you in the papers. I'll write the details of the crime and I'll not rest till you're brought to trial."

"You'll profit nothing from that," said the lieutenant with a smile. "You haven't a single piece of evidence with which to convict me. The real crime was committed by the desert. Nothing killed him but his aspiring to freedom. Freedom is the criminal which should be brought to trial. All I did was to be late, just a little late. I did that on purpose: several hours or perhaps half a day. The rest of the job the desert was able to do on my behalf. I had to do it – a small punishment in the name of authority against which he had rebelled, refusing to take the bread from its hand. As for my confessions, there is no witness except yourself and you require a third party to establish my crime, as you call it."

"But there are the locals, they'll testify in my favour. They told me of your hatred and that of the Governor and provincial officers for him; they are sympathetic towards him and will testify against you. You hate him because he knows the truth about you and I'll expose… "

"That's enough of that," the lieutenant interrupted him coldly. "Knowledge of the truth in our time is a justification that is all too sufficient for being punished. Listen – my own brother was also in opposition."

He was silent for a while as he watched the dust sweeping across the windscreen.

Then, his voice quavering, he went on:

"He was stubbornly in opposition at the beginning of independence and it wasn't long before the authorities recognised how dangerous he was. Then, all of a sudden, he disappeared."

"Disappeared?" An exclamation of surprise escaped from Misbah Said's lips.

"Yes, he disappeared from that time until today."

"Where would he have disappeared to?"

Ignoring his question, the lieutenant continued:

"That day I discovered the truth. I had to make a choice: either to keep to the truth or to ignore it forever."

"To betray your conscience?"

"Yes. I wanted to live. I chose to keep possession of my bread and butter."

"You took bread in exchange for truth," commented Misbah Said scornfully.

"And why not?"

"You betrayed your conscience."

"And why not?"

Silence rose up between them like a wall. A little later the lieutenant looked out of the window, then turned to Misbah Said and in a tone which, for the first time, was devoid of any harshness, said:

"I trust you've understood me."

He turned the switch and put his foot down on the accelerator.

IN THE CAFETERIA of Sebha Airport the two of them sat facing one another after Misbah had checked in his luggage. After a long silence he said:

"Thanks for everything."

The lieutenant remained silent, his eyes roving among the passengers.

The loudspeaker system informed passengers that they should make their way to the plane, so Misbah rose to his feet, only to find that the lieutenant was already standing in front of him, his hand held out to him as though it were a revolver. Misbah shook the hand and they exchanged a quick glance.

Before Misbah disappeared amidst the crowd of other passengers the lieutenant had caught up with him and said in a hissed whisper:

"Don't count too much on the locals," and bade him farewell with an enigmatic smile.

S M A L L   S U N

by Zakaria Tamer

Zakaria Tamer, born in Damascus in 1929, is one of the best-known short story writers in the Arab world. His stories are often allegorical with political overtones.

Translated by Denys Johnson-Davies

ABU FAHD was returning home. He walked with slow steps, swaying slightly, through the narrow winding alleys that were lit by widely scattered lamps giving out a yellow light.

The silence that reigned all round him oppressed Abu Fahd, so he began to sing in a soft lilting voice:

"Poor me, what a state I'm in!"

It was almost midnight. Abu Fahd's exultation increased, for he had drunk three glasses of arak. Again he burst out drunkenly:

"Poor me, what a state I'm in!"

It seemed to him that his raucous voice was filled with an exquisite sweetness and he told himself aloud: "I'm in fine voice."

He imagined people with mouths agape waving their hands, cheering and clapping. He laughed for a long time, then tilted his tarboosh slightly back. He resumed singing joyfully:

"Poor me, what a state I'm in!"

He was wearing grey-coloured baggy trousers and had an old yellow belt round his waist. When he arrived under the arched bridge where the darkness was stronger than the light, he was surprised to see a small black sheep standing against the wall. He opened his mouth in amazement and said to himself: "I'm not drunk. Look well, man, what do you see? It's a sheep. Where's its owner?"

He looked about him but found no one – the alley was utterly deserted. Then, staring at the sheep, he said to himself: "Am I drunk?"

He gave a low laugh and said to himself: "Allah is Munificent, He knows that Abu Fahd and Umm Fahd haven't eaten meat for a week." Abu Fahd approached the sheep and tried to force it to move along by pushing it forwards, but it refused to budge. Abu Fahd therefore seized it by its two small horns and tugged at them, but the sheep remained rigidly against the wall. Abu Fahd regarded it with fury, then said to it:

"I'll carry you off – and your mother and father too."

Abu Fahd took the sheep and lifted it up and placed it on his back, holding its two front legs in his hands, then proceeded on his way while resuming his singing, his joyous elation much increased. After a while, though, he stopped singing for he was conscious that the sheep had grown in size and weight. All of a sudden he heard a voice saying: "Let me be. "

Abu Fahd's forehead knotted into a frown and he said to himself: "May Allah curse drunkenness."

After some moments he heard the same voice saying: "Let me be, I'm not a sheep."

Abu Fahd shuddered and his terror impelled him to hold fast to the sheep. He came to a halt and the voice spoke again:

"I'm the son of the King of the Djinn. Let me be and I'll give you anything you want."

Abu Fahd didn't reply but continued on his way with hasty steps.

"I'll give you seven jars filled with gold."

Abu Fahd imagined he heard the ring of pieces of gold dropping down from some nearby place and striking the ground.

The sheep slipped from him, and he turned around just as he had been about to say: "Let's have them."

He found himself alone in the long narrow alley. He couldn't find the sheep and remained nailed to the spot for a while in terror, then continued hastily on his way. On arriving home he woke up his wife Umm Fahd and told her of what had happened.

"Go to sleep, you're drunk," she said.

"I only had three glasses."

"You get dizzy on a single glass."

Abu Fahd felt he'd been insulted, so he answered defiantly:

"I don't get dizzy on a whole barrel of arak."

Umm Fahd uttered not a word and began bringing to mind the tales she'd heard as a child about the djinn and their sport.

Abu Fahd undressed, switched off the light and stretched out beside his wife, pulling the coverlet up to his chin.

Suddenly Umm Fahd said:

"You should not have let it go before it'd given you the gold."

Abu Fahd did not answer and Umm Fahd continued with fervour:

"Go tomorrow and take hold of it and don't let it go."

Abu Fahd gave a tired, sad yawn.

"And how shall I find it?" he asked wearily.

"For certain you'll find it under the bridge. Bring it home and we won't let it go till it gives us the money."

"I won't find it."

"The djinn live by day under the ground. When night comes they go up to the earth's surface and sport there till dawn draws near. If they have come to like particular place, they continually return to it. You will find the sheep under the bridge."

Abu Fahd stretched out his hand to her bosom and thrust it between her breasts, where he left it motionless.

"We'll become rich," he said.

"We'll buy a house."

"A house with a garden."

"And we'll buy a radio."

"A large one."

"And a washing machine."

"A washing machine."

"We won't eat any more crushed wheat."

"We'll eat white bread."

Umm Fahd laughed like a child, while Abu Fahd continued: "I'll buy you a red dress."

"Just one dress?" whispered Umm Fahd in a tone of reproof.

"I'll buy you a hundred dresses."

Abu Fahd was silent for several moments, then enquired:

"When will you give birth?"

"In three months."

"It'll be a boy."

"He'll not suffer as we did."

"He won't go hungry."

"His clothes will be beautiful and clean."

"He won't have to search around for work."

"He'll study at schools."

"The owner of the house won't ask him for rent."

"He'll be a doctor when he grows up."

"I want him to be a lawyer."

"We'll ask him: Do you want to be a lawyer or a doctor?"

She clung to him tenderly and continued by enquiring in a sly tone:

"And won't you marry again?"

He gave her ear a light nip:

"Why should I marry? You're the best woman on earth."

They lapsed into silence, being immersed in a great, tranquil feeling of elation.

But after a while Abu Fahd took away the coverlet from his body with a sudden movement.

"What's wrong?" asked Umm Fahd.

"I'll go now."

"Where to?"

"I'll bring the sheep."

"Wait till tomorrow night. Sleep now."

He hurriedly left the bed, switched on the light that hung from the ceiling and began dressing.

"Maybe you won't find it."

"I'll find it."

"Be careful not to let it go," said Umm Fahd as she helped him wrap the yellow belt round his waist.

Abu Fahd felt that he was venturing upon some hazardous undertaking. He would be in need of his dagger, a dagger with embossed blade and swarthy gleam.

Leaving the house and setting off at speed till he arrived under the bridge, he was overcome by a sense of frustration when he didn't find the sheep. The alley was vacant, and the windows of the houses scattered along the two sides had their lights switched off.

Abu Fahd stood waiting, motionless, resting his back against the wall. After a while there came to his ears a noise that drew closer and presently there appeared a drunken man who was staggering and bumping against the walls of the alley, while he shouted in a drawn-out voice:

"Hey, I'm a man."

On drawing near Abu Fahd, the man came to a stop and stared in utter astonishment.

"What are you doing here?" he said in a stumbling, joyful voice.

"Get out."

The drunken man knotted his brows in thought, then his face became radiant with joy:

"By Allah, I too love women. Are you waiting for the husband to go to sleep and for the wife to open the door to you?"

Abu Fahd was annoyed; he felt his irritation growing within him as the drunken man continued what he had to say:

"Is the woman beautiful?"

"What woman?" said Abu Fahd with exasperation.

"The woman you're waiting for."

"Get out."

"I'll be your partner."

Abu Fahd's anger grew more intense, for he feared that the

sheep would not make an appearance because of the drunken man's presence.

"Get on your way or I'll break your head," he said fiercely.

The drunken man belched. "Are you ordering me about?" he said in a tone of surprise. "Who do you think you are?"

He was silent for a while, then added: "Come and break my head. Come on."

"Go away and leave me," said Abu Fahd. "I don't want to break your head."

"No, no," said the drunken man indignantly. "Come along and break my head."

He backed away slightly and said in a joyful voice:

"I'll turn you into a sieve."

The drunken man plunged his hand into his trouser pocket and extracted from it a long-bladed razor. Abu Fahd put his hand to his belt, unsheathing his dagger, while the drunken man approached him warily yet with speed.

Abu Fahd raised his dagger high and brought it down, at which the drunken man moved to the left with lightning suddenness so that the dagger didn't touch him, and thrust the razor into Abu Fahd's chest as he shouted: "Take that!"

Withdrawing the razor from the flesh, the man backed away slightly. Abu Fahd clung closely to the mud wall and raised his dagger a second time, but the drunken man's razor again stabbed him in the chest. The third time he was stabbed in the right shoulder and at once his arm dangled limply and the fingers released the dagger, which fell to the ground.

Leaping about around him, the drunken man shouted:

"Take this... and this."

He stabbed him in the waist. Abu Fahd gave a moan and his knees went weak. He tried to remain standing steadily on his feet, but the razor was launching attacks at him, striking his flesh and tearing it without relaxation.

"Take that," shouted the drunken man.

He stabbed Abu Fahd in the stomach and his entrails spilled out. Abu Fahd pressed his hands against them: they were hot, wet and quivering. He slipped and fell down. He lay sprawled on his back, while the drunken man, standing close by him, leaned over, coughed several times, vomited, then ran off.

Abu Fahd heard the sheep say to him:

"Seven jars of gold."

Much gold fell down, glittering like a small sun. Then the sound of it began to move ever further and further away.

CLOCKS LIKE HORSES

by *Mohammed Khudayyir*

Mohammed Khudayyir was born in 1940 and lives in southern Iraq near Basra, where he is a school teacher. Much of his writing draws on folklore.

Translated by Denys Johnson-Davies

T HIS MEETING may take place. I shall get my watch repaired and go out to the quays of the harbour, then at the end of the night I shall return to the hotel and find him sleeping in my bed, his face turned to the wall, having hung his red turban on the clothes hook.

Till today I still own a collection of old watches; I had come by them from an uncle of mine who used to be a sailor on the ships of the Andrew Weir company; old pocket watches with chains and silver-plated cases, all contained in a small wooden box in purses of shiny blue cloth. While my interest in them has of late waned, I had, as a schoolboy, been fascinated by them. I would take them out from their blue purses and scrutinize their workings in an attempt to discover something about them that would transcend "time stuffed like old cotton in a small cushion," as I had recorded one day in my diary.

One day during the spring school holidays I was minded to re-move one of these watches from its box and to put it into the pocket of my black suit, attaching its chain to the buttonholes of my waistcoat. For a long time I wandered round the chicken market before seating myself at a café. The waiter came and asked me the time. I calmly took the watch out of its blue purse. My watch was incapable of telling the time, like the other watches in the box, nothing in it working except for the spring of the case which was no sooner pressed than it flicked open revealing a pure white dial and two hands that stood pointing to two of the Roman numerals on the face. Before I could inform him that the watch was not working, the waiter had bent down and pulled the short chain towards him; having looked attentively at the watch he closed its case on which had been engraved a sailing ship within a frame of foreign writing. Then, giving it back to me, he stood up straight.

"How did you get hold of it?"

"I inherited it from a relative of mine."

I returned the watch to its place.

"Was your relative a sailor?"

"Yes."

"Only three or four of the famous sailors are still alive."

"My relative was called Mughamis."

"Mughamis? I don't know him."

"He wouldn't settle in one place. He died in Bahrain."

"That's sailors for you! Do you remember another sailor called Marzouk? Since putting ashore for the last time he has been living in Fao. He opened a shop there for repairing watches, having learned the craft from the Portuguese. He alone would be able to repair an old watch like yours."

I drank down the glass of tea and said to the waiter as I paid him: "Did you say he was living in Fao?"

"Yes, near the hotel."

The road to Fao is a muddy one and I went on putting off the journey until one sunny morning I took my place among the pas-sengers in a bus which set off loaded with luggage. The passengers, who sat opposite one another in the middle of the bus, exchanged no words except for general remarks about journeying in winter, about how warm this winter was, and other comments about the holes in the road. At the moment they stopped talking I took out my watch. Their eyes became fixed on it, but no one asked me about it or asked the time. Then we began to avoid looking at each other and transferred our attentions to the vast open countryside and to the distant screen of date palms in the direction of the east that kept our vehicle company and hid the villages along the Shatt al-Arab.

We arrived at noon and someone showed me to the hotel which lies at the intersection of straight roads and looks on to a square in the middle of which is a round fenced garden. The hotel consisted of two low storeys, while the balcony that overlooked the square was at such a low height that someone in the street could have climbed up on to it. I, who cannot bear the smell of hotels, or the heavy, humid shade in their hallways in daytime, hastened to call out to its owners. When I repeated my call, a boy looked down from a door at the side and said: "Do you want to sleep here?"

"Have you a place?" I said.

The boy went into the room and from it there emerged a man whom I asked for a room with a balcony. The boy who was showing me the way informed me that the hotel would be empty by day and packed at night. Just as the stairway was the shortest of stairways and the balcony the lowest of balconies, my room was the smallest and contained a solitary bed, but the sun entered it from the balcony. I threw my bag onto the bed and the boy sat down beside me. "The doors are all without locks," said the boy. "Why should we lock them – the travellers only stay for one night."

Then he leaned towards me and whispered: "Are you Indian?"

This idea came as a surprise to me. The boy himself was more likely to be Indian with his dark complexion, thick brilliantined hair and sparkling eyes. I whispered to him: "Did they tell you that Basra used to be called the crotch of India, and that the Indian invaders in the British army, who came down to the land of Fao first of all, desired no other women except those of Basra?"

The boy ignored my cryptic reference to the mixing of passions and blending of races and asked, if I wasn't Indian, where did I live?

"I've come from Ashar," I told him, "on a visit to the watchmaker. Would you direct me to him?"

"Perhaps you mean the old man who has many clocks in his house," said the boy.

"Yes, that must be he," I said.

"He's not far from the hotel," he said. "He lives alone with his daughter and never leaves the house."

The boy brought us lunch from a restaurant, and we sat on the bed to eat, and he told me about the man I had seen downstairs: "He's not the owner of the hotel, just a permanent guest."

Then, with his mouth full of food, he whispered: "He's got a pistol."

"You know a lot of things, O Indian," I said, also speaking in a whisper.

He protested that he wasn't Indian but was from Hasa. He had a father who worked on the ships that transported dates from Basra to the coastal towns of the Gulf and India.

THE BOY took me to the watchmaker, leaving me in front of the door of his house. A gap made by a slab of stone that had been removed from its place in the upper frieze of the door made this entrance unforgettable. One day, in tropical years, there had stopped near where I was a sailor shaky with sickness, or some Sikh soldier shackled with lust, and he had looked at the slab of stone on which was engraved some date or phrase, before continuing on his unknown journey. And after those two there perhaps came some foreign archaeologist whose boat had been obstructed by the silt and who had put up in the town till the water rose, and his curiosity for things Eastern had been drawn to the curves of the writing on the slab of stone and he had torn it out and carried it off with him to his boat. Now I, likewise, was in front of this gateway to the sea.

On the boy's advice I did not hesitate to push open the door and enter into what looked like a porch which the sun penetrated through apertures near the ceiling and in which I was confronted by hidden and persistent ticking sounds and a garrulous ringing that issued from the pendulums and hammers of large clocks of the type that strike the hours, ranged along the two sides of the porch. As I proceeded one or more clocks struck at the same time. All the clocks were similar in size, in the great age of the wood of their frames, and in the shape of their round dials, their Roman numerals, and their delicate arrow-like hands – except that these hands were pointing to different times.

I had to follow the slight curve of the porch to come unexpectedly upon the last of the great sailors in his den, sitting behind a large table on which was heaped the wreckage of clocks. He was occupied with taking to pieces the movement of a clock by the light of a shaded lamp that hung down from the ceiling at a height close to his frail, white-haired head. He looked towards me with a glance from one eye that was naked and another on which a magnifying-glass had been fixed, then went back to disassembling the movement piece by piece. The short glance was sufficient to link this iron face with the nuts, cogwheels and hands of the movements of the many clocks hanging on the walls and thrown into corners under dust and rust. Clocks that didn't work and others that did, the biggest of them being a clock on the wall above the watchmaker's head, which was, to be precise, the movement of a large grandfather clock made of brass, the dial of which had been removed and which had been divested of its cabinet so that time manifested itself in it naked and shining, sweeping along on its serrated cogwheels in a regular mechanical sequence: from the rotation of the spring to the pendulum that swung harmoniously to and fro and ended in the slow, tremulous, imperceptible movement of the hands. When the cogwheels had taken the hands along a set distance of time's journey, the striking cogwheel would move and raise the hammer. I had not previously seen a naked, throbbing clock and thus I became mesmerised by the regular throbbing that synchronised with the swinging motion of the pendulum and with the movement of the cogwheels of various diameters. I started at the sound of the hammer falling against the bell; the gallery rang with three strokes whose reverberations took a long time to die away, while the other clocks went on, behind the glass of their cabinets, with their incessant ticking.

The watchmaker raised his head and asked me if the large clock above his head had struck three times.

Then, immersing himself in taking the mechanism to pieces, he said: "Like horses; like horses running on the ocean bed."

A clock in the porch struck six times and he said: "Did one of them strike six times? It's six in America. They're getting up now, while the sun is setting in Burma."

Then the room was filled again with noisy reverberations. "Did it strike seven? It's night-time in Indonesia. Did you make out the last twelve strokes? They are fast asleep in the furthest west of the world. After some hours the sun will rise in the furthest east. What time is it? Three? That's our time, here near the Gulf."

One clock began striking on its own. After a while the chimes blended with the tolling of other clocks as hammers coincided in falling upon bells, and others landed halfway between the times of striking and yet others fell between these halfways so that the chimes hurried in pursuit of one another in a confused scale. Then, one after another, the hammers became still, the chimes growing further apart, till a solitary clock remained, the last clock that had not discharged all its time, letting it trickle out now in a separate, high-pitched reverberation.

He was holding my watch in his grasp. "Several clocks might strike together," he said, "strike as the fancy takes them. I haven't liked to set my clocks to the same time. I have assigned to my daughter the task of merely winding them up. They compete with one another like horses. I have clocks that I bought from people who looted them from the houses of Turkish employees who left them as they hurried away after the fall of Basra. I also got hold of clocks that were left behind later on by the Jews who emigrated. Friends of mine, the skippers of ships, who would come to visit me here, would sell me clocks of European manufacture. Do you see the clock over there in the passageway? It was in the house of the

Turkish commander of the garrison of Fao's fortress."

I saw the gleam of the quick-swinging pendulum behind glass in the darkness of the cabinets of the clocks in the porch. Then I asked him about my watch. "Your watch? It's a rare one. They're no longer made. I haven't handled such a watch for a long time. I'm not sure about it but I'll take it to pieces. Take a stroll round and come back here at night."

That was what I'd actually intended to do. I would return before night. The clocks bade me farewell with successive chimes. Four chimes in Fao: seven p.m. in the swarming streets of Calcutta. Four chimes: eight a.m. in the jungles of Buenos Aries... Outside the den the clamour had ceased, also the smell of engine oil and of old wood.

I RETURNED at sunset. I had spent the time visiting the old barracks which had been the home of the British army of occupation, then I had sat in a café near the fish market.

I didn't find the watchmaker in his former place, but presently I noticed a huge empty cabinet that had been moved into a gap between the clocks. The watchmaker was in an open courtyard before an instrument made up of clay vessels, which I guessed to be a type of water-clock. When he saw me he called out: "Come here. Come, I'll show you something."

I approached the vessels hanging on a cross-beam: from them water dripped into a vessel hanging on another, lower cross-beam; the water then flowed onto a metal plate on the ground, in which there was a gauge for measuring the height of the water.

"A water-clock?"

"Have you seen one like it?"

"I've read about them. They were the invention of people of old."

"The Persians call them *bingan*."

"I don't believe it tells the right time."

"No, it doesn't, it reckons only twenty hours to the day. According to its reckoning I'm 108 years old instead of ninety, and it is seventy-eight years since the British entered Basra instead of sixty. I learned how to make it from a Muscati sailor who had one like it in his house on the coast."

I followed him to the den, turning to two closed doors in the small courtyard on which darkness had descended. He returned the empty clock-cabinet to its place and seated himself in his chair. His many clothes lessened his appearance of senility; he was lost under his garments, one over another and yet another over them, his head inside a vast tarbush.

"I've heard you spent a lifetime at sea."

"Yes. It's not surprising that our lives are always linked to water. I was on one of the British India ships as a syce with an English trader dealing in horses."

He toyed with the remnants of the watches in front of him, then said: "He used to call himself by an Arabic name. We would call him Surour Saheb. He used to buy Nejdi horses from the rural areas of the south and they would then be shipped to Bombay where they would be collected up and sent to the racecourses in England. Fifteen days on end at sea, except that we would make stops at the Gulf ports. We would stop for some days in Muscat. When there were strong winds against us we would spend a month at sea. The captains, the cooks and the pilots were Indians, while the others, seamen and syces, were from Muscat, Hasa and Bahrain; the rest were from the islands of the Indian Ocean. We would have with us divers from Kuwait. I remember their small dark bodies and plaited hair as they washed down the horses on the shore or led them to the ship. I was the youngest syce. I began my first sea journey at the age of twelve. I joined the ship with my father who was an assistant to the captain and responsible for looking after the stores and equipment. There were three of us, counting my father, who would sleep in the storeroom among the sacks and barrels of tar, the fish oil, ropes and dried fish, on beds made up of coconut fibre."

"Did you make a lot?"

"We? We didn't make much. The trader did. Each horse would

fetch 800 rupees in Bombay, and when we had reached Bengal it would fetch 1,500 rupees. On our return to Basra we would receive our wages for having looked after the horses. Some of us would buy goods from India and sell them on our return journey wherever we put in: cloth, spices, rice, sugar, perfumes and wood, and sometimes peacocks and monkeys."

"Did you employ horses in the war?"

"I myself didn't take part in the war. Of course they used them. When the Turks prevented us from trading with them because they needed them for the army, we moved to the other side of the river. We had a corral and a caravanserai for sleeping in at Khorramshahr. From there we began to smuggle out the horses far from the clutches of the Turkish customs men. On the night when we'd be travelling we'd feed and water the horses well and at dawn we'd proceed to the corral and each syce would lead out his horse. As for me I was required to look after the transportation of the provisions and fodder; other boys who were slightly older than me were put in charge of the transportation of the water, the ropes, the chains and other equipment. The corral was close to the shore, except that the horses would make a lot of noise and stir up dust when they were being pulled along by the reins to the ship that would lie at the end of an anchorage stretching out to it from the shore. The ship would rock and tiny bits of straw would become stuck on top of our heads while the syces would call the horses by their names, telling them to keep quiet, until they finished tying them up in their places. It was no easy matter, for during the journey the waves, or the calm of the invisible sea, would excite one of the horses or would make it ill, so that its syce would have to spend the night with it, watching over it and keeping it company. As we lay in our sleeping quarters we would hear the syce reassuring his horse with some such phrase as: "Calm down. Calm down, my Precious Love. The grass over there is better." However this horse, whose name was Precious Love, died somewhere near Aden. At dawn the sailors took it up and consigned it to the waves. It was a misty morning and I was carrying a lantern, and I heard the great carcass hitting the water, though without seeing it; I did, though, see its syce's face close to me — he would be returning from his voyage without any earnings."

Two or three clocks happened to chime together. I said to him: "Used you to put in to Muscat?"

"Yes. Did I tell you about our host in Muscat? His wooden house was on the shore of a small bay, opposite an old stone fortress on the other side. We would set out for his house by boat. By birth he was a highlander, coming from the tribes in the mountains facing the bay. He was also a sorcerer. He was a close friend of Surour Saheb, supplying him with a type of ointment the Muscati used to prepare out of mountain herbs, which the Englishman would no sooner smear on his face than it turned a dark green and would gleam in the lamplight like a wave among rocks. In exchange for this the Muscati would get tobacco from him. I didn't join them in smoking, but I was fond of chewing a type of olibanum that was to be found extensively in the markets of the coast. I would climb up into a high place in the room that had been made as a permanent bed and would watch them puffing out the smoke from the *narghiles* into the air as they lay relaxing round the fire, having removed their dagger-belts and placed them in front of them alongside their coloured turbans. Their beards would be plunged in the smoke and the rings would glitter in their ears under the combed locks of hair whenever they turned towards the merchant, lost in thought. The merchant, relaxing on feather cushions, would be wearing brightly coloured trousers of Indian cloth and would be wrapped round in an *aba* of Kashmir wool; as for his silk turban, he would, like the sailors, have placed it in front of him beside his pistol."

"Did you say that the Muscati was a sorcerer?"

"He had a basket of snakes in which he would lay one of the sailors, then bring him out alive. His sparse body would be swallowed in his lustrous flowing robes, as was his small head in his saffron-coloured turban with the tassels. We were appalled at his repulsive greed for food, for he would eat a whole basketful of dates during a night and would drink enough water to provide for ten horses. He was amazing, quite remarkable; he would perform bizarre acts; swallowing a puff from his *narghile*, he would after a while begin to release the smoke from his mouth and nose for five consecutive minutes. You should have seen his stony face, with the clouds of smoke floating against it like serpents that flew and danced. He was married to seven women for whom he had dug out, in the foot of the mountain, rooms that overlooked the bay. No modesty prevented him from disclosing their fabulous names: Mountain Flower, Daylight Sun, Sea Pearl, Morning Star. He was a storehouse of spicy stories and tales of strange travels and we would draw inspiration from him for names for our horses. At the end of the night he would leave us sleeping and would climb up the mountain. At the end of one of our trips we stayed as his guest for seven nights, during which time men from the Muscati's tribe visited us to have a smoke; they would talk very little and would look with distaste at the merchant and would then leave quietly with their antiquated rifles.

"Our supper would consist of spiced rice and grilled meat or fish. We would be given a sweet sherbet to drink in brass cups. As for the almond-filled *halva* of Muscat that melts in the mouth, even the bitter coffee could not disperse its scented taste. In the morning he would return and give us some sherbet to drink that would settle our stomachs, which would be suffering from the night's food and drink, and would disperse the tobacco fumes from the sailors' heads."

An outburst of striking clocks prevented him momentarily from enlarging further. He did not wait for the sound to stop before continuing:

"On the final night of our journey he overdid his tricks in quite a frightening manner. While the syces would seek help from his magic in treating their sick horses, they were afraid nonetheless that the evil effects of his magic would spread and reap the lives of these horses. And thus it was that a violent wind drove our ship onto a rock at the entrance to the bay and smashed it. Some of us escaped drowning, but the sorcerer of Muscat was not among them. He was travelling with the ship on his way to get married to a woman from Bombay; but the high waves choked his shrieks and eliminated his magic."

"And the horses?"

"They combated the waves desperately. They were swimming in the direction of the rocky shore, horses battling against the white horses of the waves. All of them were drowned. That was my last journey in the horse ships. After that, in the few years that preceded the war, I worked on the mail ships."

He made a great effort to remember and express himself:

"In Bahrain I married a woman who bore me three daughters whom I gave in marriage to sons of the sea. I stayed on there with the boatbuilders until after the war. Then, in the thirties, I returned to Basra and bought the clocks and settled in Fao, marrying a woman from here."

"You are one of the few sailors who are still alive today."

He asked me where I lived and I told him that I had put up at the hotel. He said:

"A friend of mine used to live in it. I don't know if he's still alive – for twenty years I haven't left my house."

Then, searching among the fragments of watches, he asked me in surprise:

"Did you come to Fao just because of the watch?"

I answered him that there were some towns one had to go to. He handed me my watch. It was working. Before placing it in my hand he scrutinized its flap on which had been engraved a ship with a triangular sail, which he said was of the type known as *sunbuk*.

I opened the flap. The hands were making their slow way round. The palms of my hand closed over the watch, and we listened to the sea echoing in the clocks of the den. The slender legs of horses run in the streets of the clock faces, are abducted in the glass of the large grandfather clocks. The clocks tick and strike: resounding hooves, chimes driven forward like waves. A chime: the friction of chains and ropes against wet wood. Two chimes: the dropping of the anchor into the blue abyss. Three: the call of the rocks. Four: the storm blowing up. Five: the neighing of the horses. Six... seven... eight... nine... ten... eleven... twelve...

THIS WINDING lane is not large enough to allow a lorry to pass, but it lets in a heavy damp night and sailors leading their horses, and a man dizzy from sea-sickness, still holding in his grasp a pocket watch and making an effort to avoid the water and the gentle sloping of the lane and the way the walls curve round. The bends increase with the thickening darkness and the silence. Light seeps through from the coming bend, causing me to quicken my step. In its seeping through and the might of its radiation it seems to be marching against the wall, carving into the damp brickwork folds of skins and crumpled faces that are the masks of seamen and traders from different races who have passed by here before me and are to be distinguished only by their headgear: the bedouin of Nejd and the rural areas of the south by the *kuffiyeh* and *'iqal*, the Iraqi effendis of the towns by the *sidara*; the Persians by the black tarbooshes made of goat-skin; the Ottoman officers, soldiers and government employees by their tasselled tarbooshes; the Indians by their red turbans; the Jews by flat red tarbooshes; the monks and missionaries by their black head coverings; the European sea captains by their naval caps; the explorers in disguise... They rushed out towards the rustling noise coming from behind the last bend, the eerie rumbling, the bated restlessness of the waves below the high balustrades... Then, here are Fao's quays, the lamps leading its wooden bridges along the water for a distance; in the spaces between them boats are anchored one alongside another, their lights swaying; there is also a freighter with its lights on, anchored between the two middle berths. It was possible for me to make out in the middle of the river scattered floating lights. I didn't go very close to the quay installations but contented myself with standing in front of the dark, bare extension of the river. To my surprise a man who was perhaps working as a watchman or worker on the quays approached me and asked me for the time. Eleven.

On my return to the hotel I took a different road, passing by the closed shops. I was extremely alert. The light will be shining brightly in the hotel vestibule. The oil stove will be in the middle of it, and to one side of the vestibule will be baggage, suitcases, a watercooling box and a cupboard. Seated on the bench will be a man who is dozing, his cigarette forgotten between his fingers. It will happen that I shall approach the door of my room, shall open the door, and shall find him sleeping in my bed; he will be turned to the wall, having hung his red turban on the clothes hook.

ANOTHER EVENING AT THE CLUB

by Alifa Rifaat

Alifa Rifaat is in her late fifities and lives in Cairo
with her children. She draws much of the material
for her short stories from her experience of living
in the Egyptian countryside.

Translated by Denys Johnson-Davies

IN A STATE of tension, she awaited the return of her husband.
At a loss to predict what would happen between them, she moved
herself back and forth in the rocking chair on the wide wooden
verandah that ran along the bank and occupied part of the river itself, its supports being fixed in the river bed, while around it grew
grasses and reeds. As though to banish her apprehension, she
passed her fingers across her hair. The spectres of the eucalyptus
trees ranged along the garden fence rocked before her gaze, with
white egrets slumbering on their high branches like huge white
flowers among the thin leaves.

The crescent moon rose from behind the eastern mountains
and the peaks of the gently stirring waves glistened in its feeble
rays, intermingled with threads of light leaking from the houses of
Manfalout scattered along the opposite bank. The coloured bulbs
fixed to the trees in the garden of the club at the far end of the

town stood out against the surrounding darkness. Somewhere over there her husband now sat, most likely engrossed in a game of chess.

It was only a few years ago that she had first laid eyes on him at her father's house, meeting his gaze that weighed up her beauty and priced it before offering the dowry. She had noted his eyes ranging over her as she presented him with the coffee in the Japanese cups that were kept safely locked away in the cupboard for important guests. Her mother had herself laid them out on the silver-plated tray with its elaborately embroidered spread. When the two men had taken their coffee, her father had looked up at her with a smile and had told her to sit down, and she had seated herself on the sofa facing them, drawing the end of her dress over her knees and looking through lowered lids at the man who might choose her as his wife. She had been glad to see that he was tall, well-built and clean-shaven except for a thin greying moustache. In particular she noticed the well-cut coat of English tweed and the silk shirt with gold links. She had felt herself blushing as she saw him returning her gaze. Then the man turned to her father and took out a gold case and offered him a cigarette.

"You really shouldn't, my dear sir," said her father, patting his chest with his left hand and extracting a cigarette with trembling fingers. Before he could bring out his box of matches Abboud Bey had produced his lighter.

"No, after you, my dear sir," said her father in embarrassment. Mingled with her sense of excitement at this man who gave out such an air of worldly self-confidence was a guilty shame at her father's inadequacy.

After lighting her father's cigarette Abboud Bey sat back, crossing his legs, and took out a cigarette for himself. He tapped it against the case before putting it in the corner of his mouth and lighting it, then blew out circles of smoke that followed each other across the room.

"It's a great honour for us, my son," said her father, smiling first at Abboud Bey, then at his daughter, at which Abboud Bey looked across at her and asked:

"And the beautiful little girl's still at secondary school?"

She lowered her head modestly and her father had answered:

"As from today she'll be staying at home in readiness for your happy life together, Allah permitting," and at a glance from her father she had hurried off to join her mother in the kitchen.

"You're a lucky girl," her mother had told her. "He's a real find. Any girl would be happy to have him. He's an Inspector of Irrigation though he's not yet forty. He earns a big salary and gets a fully furnished government house wherever he's posted, which will save us the expense of setting up a house – and I don't have to tell you what our situation is – and that's besides the house he owns in Alexandria where you'll be spending your holidays."

Samia had wondered to herself how such a splendid suitor had found his way to her door. Who had told him that Mr. Mahmoud Barakat, a mere clerk at the Court of Appeal, had a beautiful daughter of good reputation?

The days were then taken up with going the rounds of Cairo's shops and choosing clothes for the new grand life she would be living. This was made possible by her father borrowing on the security of his government pension. Abboud Bey, on his part, never visited her without bringing a present. For her birthday, just before they were married, he bought her an emerald ring that came in a plush box bearing the name of a well-known jeweller in Kasr el-Nil Street. On her wedding night, as he put a diamond bracelet round her wrist, he had reminded her that she was marrying someone with a brilliant career in front of him and that one of the most important things in life was the opinion of others, particularly one's equals and seniors. Though she was still only a young girl she must try to act with suitable dignity.

"Tell people you're from the well-known Barakat family and that your father was a judge," and he went up to her and gently patted her cheeks in a fatherly, reassuring gesture that he was often to repeat during their times together.

Then, yesterday evening, she had returned from the club somewhat light-headed from the bottle of beer she had been required to drink on the occasion of someone's birthday. Her husband, noting the state she was in, hurriedly took her back home. She had undressed and put on her nightgown, leaving her jewellery on the dressing-table, and was fast asleep seconds after getting into bed. The following morning, fully recovered, she slept late, then rang the bell as usual and had breakfast brought to her. It was only as she was putting her jewellery away in the wooden and mother-of-pearl box that she realized her emerald ring was missing.

Could it have dropped from her finger at the club? In the car on the way back? No, she distinctly remembered it last thing at night, remembered the usual difficulty she had in getting it off her finger. She stripped the bed of its sheets, turned over the mattress, looked inside the pillow cases, crawled on hands and knees under the bed. The tray of breakfast lying on the small bedside table caught her eye and she remembered the young servant coming in that morning with it, remembered the noise of the tray being put down, the curtains being drawn, the tray then being lifted up again and placed on the bedside table. No one but the servant had entered the room. Should she call her and question her?

Eventually, having taken two aspirins, she decided to do nothing and await the return of her husband from work.

Directly he arrived she told him what had happened and he took her by the arm and seated her down beside him:

"Let's just calm down and go over what happened."

She repeated, this time with further details, the whole story.

"And you've looked for it?"

"Everywhere. Every possible and impossible place in the bedroom and the bathroom. You see, I remember distinctly taking it off last night."

He grimaced at the thought of last night, then said:

"Anybody been in the room since Gazia when she brought in the breakfast?"

"Not a soul. I've even told Gazia not to do the room today."

"And you've not mentioned anything to her?"

"I thought I'd better leave it to you."

"Fine, go and tell her I want to speak to her. There's no point in your saying anything but I think it would be as well if you were present when I talk to her."

Five minutes later Gazia, the young servant girl they had recently employed, entered behind her mistress. Samia took herself to a far corner of the room while Gazia stood in front of Abboud Bey, her hands folded across her chest, her eyes lowered.

"Yes, sir?"

"Where's the ring?"

"What ring are you talking about, sir?"

"Now don't make out you don't know. The one with the green stone. It would be better for you if you hand it over and then nothing more need be said."

"May Allah blind me if I've set eyes on it."

He stood up and gave her a sudden slap on the face. The girl reeled back, put one hand to her cheek, then lowered it again to her chest and made no answer to any of Abboud's questions. Finally he said to her:

"You've got just fifteen seconds to say where you've hidden the ring or else, I swear to you, you're not going to have a good time of it."

As he lifted up his arm to look at his watch the girl flinched slightly but continued in her silence. When he went to the telephone Samia raised her head and saw that the girl's cheeks were wet with tears. Abboud Bey got through to the Superintendent of Police and told him briefly what had occurred.

"Of course I haven't got any actual proof but seeing that no one else entered the room, it's obvious she's pinched it. Anyway I'll leave the matter in your capable hands – I know your people have their ways and means."

He gave a short laugh, then listened for a while and said: "I'm really most grateful to you."

He put down the receiver and turned round to Samia:

"That's it, my dear. There's nothing more to worry about. The Superintendent has promised me we'll get it back. The patrol car's on the way."

THE FOLLOWING day, in the late afternoon, she'd been sitting in front of her dressing-table rearranging her jewellery in its box when an earring slipped from her grasp and fell to the floor. As she bent to pick it up she saw the emerald ring stuck between the leg of table and the wall. Since that moment she had sat in a state of panic awaiting her husband's return from the club. She even felt tempted to walk down to the water's edge and throw it into the river so as to be rid of the unpleasantness that lay ahead.

At the sound of the screech of tyres rounding the house to the garage, she slipped the ring onto her finger. As he entered she stood up and raised her hand to show him the ring. Quickly, trying to choose her words but knowing that she was expressing herself clumsily, she explained what an extraordinary thing it was that it should have lodged itself between the dressing-table and the wall, what an extraordinary coincidence she should have dropped the earring and so seen it, how she'd thought of ringing him at the club to tell him the good news but...

She stopped in mid-sentence when she saw his frown and added weakly: "I'm sorry. I can't think how it could have happened. What do we do now?"

He shrugged his shoulders as though in surprise.

"Are you asking me, my dear lady? Nothing of course."

"But they've been beating up the girl – you yourself said they'd not let her be till she confessed."

Unhurriedly, he sat himself down as though to consider this new aspect of the matter. Taking out his case, he tapped a cigarette against it in his accustomed manner, then moistened his lips, put the cigarette in place and lit it. The smoke rings hovered in the still air as he looked at his watch and said:

"In any case she's not got all that long before they let her go. They can't keep her for more than forty-eight hours without getting any evidence or a confession. It won't kill her to put up with things for a while longer. By now the whole town knows the servant stole the ring – or would you like me to tell everyone: "Look, folks, the fact is that the wife got a bit tiddly on a couple of sips of beer and the ring took off on its own and hid itself behind the dressing-table."? What do you think?"

"I know the situation's a bit awkward... "

"Awkward? It's downright ludicrous. Listen, there's nothing to be done but to give it to me and the next time I go down to Cairo I'll sell it and get something else in its place. We'd be the laughing-stock of the town."

He stretched out his hand and she found herself taking off the ring and placing it in the outstretched palm. She was careful that their eyes should not meet. For a moment she was on the point of protesting and in fact uttered a few words:

"I'd just like to say we could... "

Putting the ring away in his pocket, he bent over her and with both hands gently patted her on the cheeks. It was a gesture she had long become used to, a gesture that promised her continued security, that told her that this man who was her husband and the father of her child had also taken the place of her father who, as though assured that he had found her a suitable substitute, had followed up her marriage with his own funeral. The gesture told her more eloquently than any words that he was the man, she the woman, he the one who carried the responsibilities, made the decisions, she the one whose role it was to be beautiful, happy, carefree. Now, though, for the first time in their life together the gesture came like a slap in the face.

Directly he removed his hands her whole body was seized with an uncontrollable trembling. Frightened he would notice, she rose to her feet and walked with deliberate steps towards the large window. She leaned her forehead against the comforting cold surface and closed her eyes tightly for several seconds. When she opened them she noticed that the café lights strung between the trees on the opposite shore had been turned on and that there were men seated under them and a waiter moving among the tables. The dark shape of a boat momentarily blocked out the café scene; in the light from the hurricane lamp hanging from its bow she saw it cutting through several of those floating islands of Nile waterlilies that, rootless, are swept along with the current.

Suddenly she became aware of his presence alongside her.

"Why don't you go and change quickly while I take the car out? It's hot and it would be nice to have supper at the club."

"As you like. Why not?"

By the time she had turned round from the window she was smiling.

T H E   V E T E R A N

by Henri Lopes

Henri Lopes, born in 1937 in Kinshasa, the Congo, has held many top-level positions in the Congo-Brazzaville government, including that of prime minister. He won the *Gran Prix Litteraire de l'Afrique Noire* in 1972. He lives in Paris and works for UNESCO.

Translated from the French
by Andrea Leskes

IT W A S not long long after the *coup d'état* that I realized the young officers were cheating on us. True, they were the ones who had urged us to participate in the conspiracy against President Takana[1], and we hadn't thought twice about risking our necks in preparing the coup. In point of fact, I had been easy to convince. I hadn't asked for a penny. The atmosphere, after three years of Takana's regime, was unbearable. Although officially the government included representatives from all the regions and ethnic groups of the country, in reality an inner circle from his tribe, including the Minister of the Interior, were the ones who actually wielded the power, advising the president on his daily decisions. Since my tribe has always ruled over Takana's, I saw my participation in the rebellion as a duty. The militia that fought against

---

1. Fictitious character.

those idiots who objected to paying taxes and performing the menial tasks ordered by the French commanders was, from the time of the white man's arrival, always conscripted from my region of the country. And I am the son and the grandson of a chief. From childhood on, the members of my family were taught to be leaders. Whereas this Takana – may he rot in prison where we've thrown him – is the son of a slave. He was brought up by a family I know and was allowed by them to learn to read and write. His lower class mentality is what drove him to play for such large stakes and contributed to his downfall.

Each pleasure was new to him. For example, he absolutely adored women. Single or married, he wanted them all to parade through his bed. He considered it his exclusive right to deflower all the young, stunning and more desirable female citizens. Once at a cocktail party he was literally bewitched by a young, beautiful stranger. She was wearing a long, white, flowing Senegalese *boubou* that evening, and seemed to have been moulded by the hands of the most skilled craftsman. He asked for an introduction. She was the wife of a young lieutenant who had just returned home. Takana did everything he could, used all the influence of his position, to convince her to accept his attentions. Nothing swayed her. In anger, he arranged for her husband to be trans-ferred to the bush, 800 miles from the capital. Finally he dis-covered a plot in which the lieutenant could be implicated. He summoned the woman and renewed his requests, offering in ex-change the freedom of her husband. It is said she slapped him in the face. In his rage, he threatened to execute the man, but did not have time to carry out his order. Our coup happened to succeed in time.

At first I was named Minister of Defence. You should have seen how I was applauded. I must admit I greatly enjoyed participating in parades, surrounded by an escort on motorcycles. None of the young men in the Revolutionary Liberation Council or in the gov-ernment possessed my natural physical presence. You can imme-diately see by the carriage of a man if he is destined to lead. Small talk, both at Council meetings or in the government, quickly bored me. Our country doesn't need frivolity, but rather a strong, energetic man. Yes, a man like me, who knows how to give orders and who, flanked by the army, would put everyone to work. Our country needs to be militarised because, as the white men say, we care too much for talk and not enough for work.

I had already planned out my entire strategy. From Chad I would bring in former Sara sharpshooters as technical assistants to our army. They would oversee the work of all the niggers. I would install loud speakers in each town, in each street, to broadcast my orders. Everyone who refused to obey would be punished by the Sara militia. Second offenders would simply be done away with. In this way everyone would march in step with my rhythm: one, two, one, two... In a few years we would surge ahead.

But as I already said, those youngsters cheated on me. While I was preparing to leave on a diplomatic mission to France and a meeting with the General to request his support (I would have been made a general and, between equals, we would have understood each other completely), they reshuffled the government and sent me as ambassador here, to Algeria, a country where I had fought on the side of the French and won honours in the French army.

What a bitter pill to swallow! For four years I had fought against the *fellahin*, the Algerian nationals, just as I had previously fought in Morocco and Tunisia. There, in fact, is where I earned my stripes. Here, in official speeches and in private conversation, all everyone talks about are the days of resistance against the French, of the *maquis* resistance fighters, and so on and so forth.

I finally began adjusting to my situation. One day I confided in the French ambassador. He understood my feelings perfectly and explained how we should leave the past behind. Wasn't it even harder for him? He introduced me into new circles, to French people and diplomats, so that finally I came to prefer life here to life in our provincial capital.

And oh, how I love the city of Algiers. It's a true metropolis, with tall houses and wide streets, full of carts and people. I'm partial to large modern cities, bustling with life, where one is just another face in the crowd. Dakar, Abidjan, Kinshasa – those are real capital cities. You know, if I were in power (maybe it will still come one day) I would ask the Americans to beautify our capital too. I would entice rich white men from around the world to open large stores like those in Paris.

And – oh yes – Algiers has its share of beautiful women. Let me tell you! That's important! Before my wife arrived I met one. Wow! You should see her. Her name is Nadia. She reminds me of some of the mulatto women at home, with her golden, willow-coloured, varnished skin. But our mulattos don't have such straight, soft hair. And her eyes are so black she needs no make-up. Her way of looking at people is what first caught my eye.

For six months now I have been seeing her. Last Saturday I promised to take her dancing at Tipaza. She mentioned that a Congolese orchestra was booked there for the season. You know how those people are masters of the art. How could I refuse? And when she looks at me, I can't deny her anything. I concocted a story about a formal bachelors' dinner in order to leave my wife at home.

We danced until two in the morning. Then we went to a hotel where I had reserved a room. At about three o'clock I said to her:

"Hey my little dove, are you asleep?"

"Dove! Why do you call me that?"

"For no special reason."

She put her head back down on my shoulder. But I could feel her tension. Then something wet touched my chest. At first I thought it was the sweat dripping from our touching bodies. But soon it was undeniable: she was crying.

"What's the matter?"

No answer. She couldn't possibly be angry with me. Never before had I been as gentle with a woman as with Nadia. She had been so happy a moment earlier.

Did her tears mean she knew our love was a dead end, despite the special chemistry between us? It was unfair to ask her if that were the problem. I began kissing her all over, caressing her straight, soft, silky hair in which my fingers always found such pleasure. Finally she broke away and sat up on the edge of the bed.

"No, it's nothing. It's not your fault. Only – my mother used to call me her little dove."

"Did you love your mother?"

"Yes, of course."

"She's no longer alive?"

"Nadia told me the circumstances of her mother's death. She herself had attended school in Oran. Her father led an arm of the National Liberation Front in her native region of Saïda. His *nom-de-guerre* had been Lightning Moustapha. Shortly before independence, the French secured precise information on him. One day they picked up her mother for questioning. They took her to prison and tried to pressure her into denouncing her husband or someone else in the movement.

"She was a remarkable woman endowed with exceptional courage. She wouldn't betray my father. I only learned of her arrest on Saturday when I came home for the weekend. When I returned to school I was crushed. I couldn't work in that place full of French girls, supporters of the same people who, at the very moment, were torturing my mother. But yet I was proud of being the daughter of a heroine. After one month they released her. They didn't press charges against her. But she had changed. Previously so beautiful and fresh, she had become white-haired and wrinkled. After her release from prison, I didn't return to school again. My mother arranged to have me evacuated to Morocco and went herself into the mountains. Not as a nurse but as a combatant. She died with a gun in her hand, in a fight against the French imperialist army."

"In the Saïda region?" I asked.

"Yes."

"In what year?"

"1960." And she told me the month.

I got up and dressed. Nadia is one of the few people in Algeria who don't know I had seen combat in the country. But I, too, can't forget that fight against the *fellahin* in 1960. They fought well and were all killed. And yes, there had been a woman among the dead.

Nadia, I will never see you again. I can no longer carry on anything but the most superficial conversation with people in this country, because I always fear stumbling on a relative or close friend of someone I killed or ordered killed.

Oh, how I long to be relieved of my post.

THE RAIN CAME

by Grace Ogot

Grace Ogot was born in 1930 in Kenya. She is a founding chairperson of the Writer's Association of Kenya. Her work includes novels and short stories.

T HE CHIEF was still far from the gate when his daughter Oganda saw him. She ran to meet him. Breathlessly she asked her father, "What is the news, great Chief? Everyone in the village is anxiously waiting to hear when it will rain." Labong'o held out his hands for his daughter but he did not say a word. Puzzled by her father's cold attitude Oganda ran back to the village to warn the others that the chief was back.

The atmosphere in the village was tense and confused. Everyone moved aimlessly and fussed in the yard without actually doing any work. A young woman whispered to her co-wife, "If they have not solved this rain business today, the chief will crack." They had watched him getting thinner and thinner as the people kept on pestering him. "Our cattle lie dying in the fields," they reported. "Soon it will be our children and then ourselves. Tell us what to do to save our lives, oh great Chief." So the chief had daily prayed with the Almighty through the ancestors to deliver them from their distress.

Instead of calling the family together and giving them the news immediately, Labong'o went to his own hut, a sign that he was not to be disturbed. Having replaced the shutter, he sat in the dimly lit hut to contemplate.

It was no longer a question of being the chief of hunger-stricken people that weighed Labong'o's heart. It was the life of his only daughter that was at stake. At the time when Oganda came to meet him, he saw the glittering chain shining around her waist. The prophecy was complete. "It is Oganda, Oganda, my only daughter, who must die so young." Labong'o burst into tears before finishing the sentence. The chief must not weep. Society had declared him the bravest of men. But Labong'o did not care any more. He assumed the position of a simple father and wept bitterly. He loved his people, the Luo, but what were the Luo for him without Oganda? Her life had brought a new life in Labong'o's world and he ruled better than he could remember. How would the spirit of the village survive his beautiful daughter? "There are so many homes and so many parents who have daughters. Why choose this one? She is all I have." Labong'o spoke as if the ancestors were there in the hut and he could see them face to face. Perhaps they were there, warning him to remember his promise on the day he was enthroned when he said aloud, before the elders, "I will lay down life, if necessary, and the life of my household, to save this tribe from the hands of the enemy." "Deny! Deny!" he could hear the voice of his forefathers mocking him.

When Labong'o was consecrated chief he was only a young man. Unlike his father, he ruled for many years with only one wife. But people rebuked him because his only wife did not bear him a daughter. He married a second, a third, and a fourth wife. But they all gave birth to male children. When Labong'o married a fifth wife she bore him a daughter. They called her Oganda, meaning "beans," because her skin was very fair. Out of Labong'o's twenty children, Oganda was the only girl. Though she was the chief's favourite, her mother's co-wives swallowed their jealous feelings and showered her with love. After all, they said, Oganda was a female child whose days in the royal family were numbered. She would soon marry at a tender age and leave the enviable position to someone else.

Never in his life had he been faced with such an impossible decision. Refusing to yield to the rainmaker's request would mean sacrificing the whole tribe, putting the interests of the individual above those of the society. More than that. It would mean disobeying the ancestors, and most probably wiping the Luo people from the surface of the earth. On the other hand, to let Oganda die as a ransom for the people would permanently cripple Labong'o spiritually. He knew he would never be the same chief again.

The words of Ndithi, the medicine man, still echoed in his ears. "Podho, the ancestor of the Luo, appeared to me in a dream last night, and he asked me to speak to the chief and the people," Ndithi had said to the gathering of tribesmen. "A young woman who has not known a man must die so that the country may have rain. While Podho was still talking to me, I saw a young woman standing at the lakeside, her hands raised, above her head. Her skin was as fair as the skin of young deer in the wilderness. Her tall slender figure stood like a lonely reed at the river bank. Her sleepy eyes wore a sad look like that of a bereaved mother. She wore a gold ring on her left ear, and a glittering brass chain around her waist. As I still marvelled at the beauty of this young woman, Podho told me, 'Out of all the women in this land, we have chosen this one. Let her offer herself a sacrifice to the lake monster! And on that day, the rain will come down in torrents. Let everyone stay at home on that day, lest he be carried away by the floods.'"

Outside there was a strange stillness, except for the thirsty birds that sang lazily on the dying trees. The blinding mid-day heat had forced the people to retire to their huts. Not far away from the chief's hut, two guards were snoring away quietly. Labong'o removed his crown and the large eagle-head that hung loosely on his shoulders. He left the hut, and instead of asking Nyabog'o the messenger to beat the drum, he went straight and beat it himself.

In no time the whole household had assembled under the siala tree where he usually addressed them. He told Oganda to wait a while in her grandmother's hut.

When Labong'o stood to address his household, his voice was hoarse and the tears choked him. He started to speak, but words refused to leave his lips. His wives and sons knew there was great danger. Perhaps their enemies had declared war on them. Labong'o's eyes were red, and they could see he had been weeping. At last he told them. "One whom we love and treasure must be taken away from us. Oganda is to die." Labong'o's voice was so faint, that he could not hear it himself. But he continued, "The ancestors have chosen her to be offered as a sacrifice to the lake monster in order that we may have rain."

They were completely stunned. As a confused murmur broke out, Oganda's mother fainted and was carried off to her own hut. But the other people rejoiced. They danced around singing and chanting, "Oganda is the lucky one to die for the people. If it is to save the people, let Oganda go."

In her grandmother's hut Oganda wondered what the whole family was discussing about her that she could not hear. Her grandmother's hut was well away from the chief's court and, much as she strained her ears, she could not hear what was said. "It must be marriage," she concluded. It was an accepted custom for the family to discuss their daughter's future marriage behind her back. A faint smile played on Oganda's lips as she thought of the several young men who swallowed saliva at the mere mention of her name.

There was Kech, the son of a neighbouring clan elder. Kech was very handsome. He had sweet, meek eyes and a roaring laughter. He would make a wonderful father, Oganda thought. But they would not be a good match. Kech was a bit too short to be her husband. It would humiliate her to have to look down at Kech each time she spoke to him. Then she thought of Dimo, the tall young man who had already distinguished himself as a brave warrior and an outstanding wrestler. Dimo adored Oganda, but Oganda thought he would make a cruel husband, always quarrelling and ready to fight. No, she did not like him. Oganda fingered the glittering chain on her waist as she thought of Osinda. A long time ago when she was quite young Osinda had given her that chain, and instead of wearing it around her neck several times, she wore it round her waist where it could stay permanently. She heard her heart pounding so loudly as she thought of him. She whispered, "Let it be you they are discussing, Osinda, the lovely one. Come now and take me away... "

The lean figure in the doorway startled Oganda who was rapt in thought about the man she loved. "You have frightened me, Grandma," said Oganda laughing. "Tell me, is it my marriage you were discussing? You can take it from me that I won't marry any of them." A smile played on her lips again. She was coaxing the old lady to tell her quickly, to tell her they were pleased with Osinda.

In the open space outside the excited relatives were dancing and singing. They were coming to the hut now, each carrying a gift to put at Oganda's feet. As their singing got nearer Oganda was able to hear what they were saying: "If it is to save the people, if it is to give us rain, let Oganda go. Let Oganda die for her people, and for her ancestors." Was she mad to think that they were singing about her? How could she die? She found the lean figure of her grandmother barring the door. She could not get out. The look on her grandmother's face warned her that there was danger around the corner. "Mother, it is not marriage then?" Oganda asked urgently. She suddenly felt panicky like a mouse cornered by a hungry cat. Forgetting that there was only one door in the hut Oganda fought desperately to find another exit. She must fight for her life. But there was none.

She closed her eyes, leapt like a wild tiger through the door, knocking her grandmother flat to the ground. There outside in mourning garments Labong'o stood motionless, his hands folded at the back. He held his daughter's hand and led her away from the excited crowd to the little red-painted hut where her mother was resting. Here he broke the news officially to his daughter.

For a long time the three souls who loved one another dearly sat in darkness. It was no good speaking. And even if they tried, the words could not have come out. In the past they had been like three cooking stones, sharing their burdens. Taking Oganda away from them would leave two useless stones which would not hold a cooking-pot.

News that the beautiful daughter of the chief was to be sacrificed to give the people rain spread across the country like wind. At sunset the chief's village was full of relatives and friends who had come to congratulate Oganda. Many more were on their way coming, carrying their gifts. They would dance till morning to keep her company. And in the morning they would prepare her a big farewell feast. All these relatives thought it a great honour to be selected by the spirits to die, in order that the society may live. "Oganda's name will always remain a living name among us," they boasted.

But was it maternal love that prevented Minya from rejoicing with the other women? Was it the memory of the agony and pain of child-birth that made her feel so sorrowful? Or was it the deep warmth and understanding that passes between a suckling babe and her mother that made Oganda part of her life, her flesh? Of course it was an honour, a great honour, for her daughter to be chosen to die for the country. But what could she gain once her only daughter was blown away by the wind? There were so many other women in the land, why choose her daughter, her only child! Had human life any meaning at all – other women had houses full of children while she, Minya, had to lose her only child!

In the cloudless sky the moon shone brightly, and the numerous stars glittered with a bewitching beauty. The dancers of all age-groups assembled to dance before Oganda, who sat close to her mother, sobbing quietly. All these years she had been with her people she thought she understood them. But now she discovered that she was a stranger among them. If they loved her as they had always professed why were they not making any attempt to save her? Did her people really understand what it felt like to die young? Unable to restrain her emotions any longer, she sobbed loudly as her age-group got up to dance. They were young and beautiful and very soon they would marry and have their own children. They would have husbands to love and little huts for them-selves. They would have reached maturity. Oganda touched the chain around her waist as she thought of Osinda. She wished Osinda were there too, among her friends. "Perhaps he is ill," she thought gravely. The chain comforted Oganda – she would die with it around her waist and wear it in the underground world.

In the morning a big feast was prepared for Oganda. The women prepared many different tasty dishes so that she could pick and choose. "People don't eat after death," they said. Deli-cious though the food looked, Oganda touched none of it. Let the happy people eat. She contented herself with sips of water from a little calabash.

The time for her departure was drawing near, and each minute was precious. It was a day's journey to the lake. She was to walk all night, passing through the great forest. But nothing could touch her, not even the denizens of the forest. She was already anointed with sacred oil. From the time Oganda received the sad news she had expected Osinda to appear any moment. But he was not there. A relative told her that Osinda was away on a private visit. Oganda realised that she would never see her beloved again.

In the afternoon the whole village stood at the gate to say good-bye and to see her for the last time. Her mother wept on her neck for a long time. The great chief in a mourning skin came to the gate bare-footed, and mingled with the people – a simple father in grief. He took off his wrist bracelet and put it on his daughter's wrist saying, "You will always live among us. The spirit of our fore-fathers is with you."

Tongue-tied and unbelieving Oganda stood there before the people. She had nothing to say. She looked at her home once more. She could hear her heart beating so painfully within her. All her childhood plans were coming to an end. She felt like a flower nipped in the bud never to enjoy the morning dew again. She looked at her weeping mother, and whispered, "Whenever you want to see me, always look at the sunset. I will be there."

Oganda turned southwards to start her trek to the lake. Her

parents, relatives, friends, and admirers stood at the gate and watched her go.

Her beautiful slender figure grew smaller and smaller till she mingled with the thin dry trees in the forest. As Oganda walked the lonely path that wound its way in the wilderness, she sang a song, and her own voice kept her company.

> The ancestors have said Oganda must die.
> The daughter of the chief must be sacrificed,
> When the lake monster feeds on my flesh.
> The people will have rain.
> Yes, the rain will come down in torrents.
> And the floods will wash away the sandy beaches
> When the daughter of the chief dies in the lake.
> My age-group has consented
> My parents have consented
> So have my friends and relatives.
> Let Oganda die to give us rain.
> My age-group are young and ripe,
> Ripe for womanhood and motherhood
> But Oganda must die young,
> Oganda must sleep with the ancestors.
> Yes, rain will come down in torrents.

The red rays of the setting sun embraced Oganda, and she looked like a burning candle in the wilderness.

The people who came to hear her sad song were touched by her beauty. But they all said the same thing: "If it is to save the people, if it is to give us rain, then be not afraid. Your name will forever live among us."

At midnight Oganda was tired and weary. She could walk no more. She sat under a big tree, and having sipped water from her calabash, she rested her head on the tree trunk and slept.

When Oganda woke up in the morning the sun was high in the sky. After walking for many hours, she reached the *tong'*, a strip of land that separated the inhabited part of the country from the sacred place (*kar lamo*). No layman could enter this place and come out alive – only those who had direct contact with the spirits and the Almighty were allowed to enter this holy of holies. But Oganda had to pass through this sacred land on her way to the lake, which she had to reach at sunset.

A large crowd gathered to see her for the last time. Her voice was now hoarse and painful, but there was no need to worry any more. Soon she would not have to sing. The crowd looked at Oganda sympathetically, mumbling words she could not hear. But none of them pleaded for life. As Oganda opened the gate, a child, a young child, broke loose from the crowd, and ran towards her. The child took a small earring from her sweaty hands and gave it to Oganda saying, "When you reach the world of the dead, give this earring to my sister. She died last week. She forgot this ring." Oganda, taken aback by the strange request, took the little ring, and handed her precious water and food to the child. She did not need them now. Oganda did not know whether to laugh or cry. She had heard mourners sending their love to their sweethearts, long dead, but this idea of sending gifts was new to her.

Oganda held her breath as she crossed the barrier to enter the sacred land. She looked appealingly at the crowd, but there was no response. Their minds were too preoccupied with their own survival. Rain was the precious medicine they were longing for, and the sooner Oganda could get to her destination the better.

A strange feeling possessed Oganda as she picked her way in the sacred land. There were strange noises that often startled her, and her first reaction was to take to her heels. But she remembered that she had to fulfil the wish of her people. She was exhausted, but the path was still winding. Then suddenly the path ended on sandy land. The water had retreated miles away from the shore leaving a wide stretch of sand. Beyond this was the vast expanse of water.

Oganda felt afraid. She wanted to picture the size and shape of the monster, but fear would not let her. The society did not talk about it, nor did the crying children who were silenced by the mention of its name. The sun was still up, but it was no longer hot. For a long time Oganda walked ankle-deep in the sand. She was exhausted and longed desperately for her calabash of water. As she moved on, she had a strange feeling that something was following her. Was it the monster? Her hair stood erect, and a cold paralysing feeling ran along her spine. She looked behind, sideways and in front, but there was nothing, except a cloud of dust.

Oganda pulled up and hurried but the feeling did not leave her, and her whole body became saturated with perspiration.

The sun was going down fast and the lake shore seemed to move along with it.

Oganda started to run. She must be at the lake before sunset. As she ran she heard a noise coming from behind. She looked back sharply, and something resembling a moving bush was frantically running after her. It was about to catch up with her.

Oganda ran with all her strength. She was now determined to throw herself into the water even before sunset. She did not look back, but the creature was upon her. She made an effort to cry out, as in a nightmare, but she could not hear her own voice. The creature caught up with Oganda. In the utter confusion, as Oganda came face with the unidentified creature, a strong hand grabbed her. But she fell flat on the sand and fainted.

When the lake breeze brought her back to consciousness, a man was bending over her. ". . . . . !" Oganda opened her mouth to speak, but she had lost her voice. She swallowed a mouthful of water poured into her mouth by the stranger.

"Osinda, Osinda! Please let me die. Let me run, the sun is going down. Let me die, let them have rain." Osinda fondled the glittering chain around Oganda's waist and wiped the tears from her face.

"We must escape quickly to the unknown land," Osinda said urgently. "We must run away from the wrath of the ancestors and the retaliation of the monster."

"But the curse is upon me, Osinda, I am no good to you any

more. And moreover the eyes of the ancestors will follow us everywhere and bad luck will befall us. Nor can we escape from the monster."

Oganda broke loose, afraid to escape, but Osinda grabbed her hands again.

"Listen to me, Oganda! Listen! Here are two coats!" He then covered the whole of Oganda's body, except her eyes, with a leafy attire made from the twigs of *Bwombwe*. "These will protect us from the eyes of the ancestors and the wrath of the monster. Now let us run out of here." He held Oganda's hand and they ran from the sacred land, avoiding the path that Oganda had followed.

The bush was thick, and the long grass entangled their feet as they ran. Halfway through the sacred land they stopped and looked back. The sun was almost touching the surface of the water. They were frightened. They continued to run, now faster, to avoid the sinking sun.

"Have faith, Oganda – that thing will not reach us."

When they reached the barrier and looked behind them trembling, only a tip of the sun could be seen above the water's surface.

"It is gone! It is gone!" Oganda wept, hiding her face in her hands.

"Weep not, daughter of the chief. Let us run, let us escape."

There was a bright lightning. They looked up, frightened. Above them black furious clouds started to gather. They began to run. Then the thunder roared, and the rain came down in torrents.

Text and cover design by Tree Swenson
The text type is Baskerville, set by The Typeworks
Manufactured by Edwards Brothers
on acid-free paper